"So show me what you've got," Nick whispered

Isabel shuddered even as she began to unbutton her blouse. "What do you want? Proof that I'll keep you warm at night?"

The garment fell open and Nick was staring down at nicely shaped breasts beneath a see-through teddy. His heart pumped faster. His mouth went drier. His erection grew harder.

Determined to push her to the edge from which she would flee, he pressed against her back and cupped her breasts from behind. He thumbed her already aroused nipples through the thin material and she arched against him.

A small gasp suddenly escaped her and Nick flushed so hot he felt burned. Her sexual response to him was triggering long-repressed memories.

They'd been younger then and innocent in their lovemaking. The vivid recollections were overpowering. Nick pulled away from her too-tempting flesh. He had to regain his composure.

Isabel swung around and faced him. "Well?" she asked coolly, the imm_____ ago gone. "Did I pa____

Dear Reader,

How exciting is this—my second CHICAGO HEAT entry in the Blaze line! The erotic thrills and chills you'll find in *Improper Conduct* go beyond the Intrigue stories I usually write for Harlequin.

I love using the hot and hip Wicker Park/Bucktown neighborhood in Chicago as my setting—also the setting of my new Intrigue series, which debuts next spring. Don't be surprised to find familiar faces and places there.

In the meantime, enjoy *Improper Conduct*, Nick's story, one of the most challenging I have ever written. Watch for Helen's story next year, the last of the CHICAGO HEAT trilogy.

Let me know what you think about *Improper Conduct*: Patricia Rosemoor, P.O. Box 578297, Chicago, IL 60657-8297 or better yet, e-mail Patricia@PatriciaRosemoor.com—and check out my Web site at www.PatriciaRosemoor.com.

Happy reading,

Patricia Rosemoor

P.S. Don't forget to check out www.tryblaze.com!

Books by Patricia Rosemoor

HARLEQUIN BLAZE
35—SHEER PLEASURE *Chicago Heat, Bk 1*

IMPROPER CONDUCT

Patricia Rosemoor

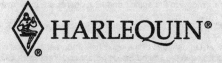

TORONTO • NEW YORK • LONDON
AMSTERDAM • PARIS • SYDNEY • HAMBURG
STOCKHOLM • ATHENS • TOKYO • MILAN • MADRID
PRAGUE • WARSAW • BUDAPEST • AUCKLAND

To my agent Jenn Jackson:
Thanks for all your hard work
and dedication on all my projects

ISBN 0-373-79059-7

IMPROPER CONDUCT

Visit us at www.eHarlequin.com

Printed in U.S.A.

1

ISABEL GRAYSON...WELL, if just seeing her name didn't make his day.

Nick Novak had taken up residence in Helen's Cybercafé, a trendy establishment painted in crackled pale yellow and furnished with overstuffed sofas and chairs. He was sitting near a fireplace at one of the computers lined up against a wall to have his Internet fix along with his morning coffee. His hard drive had crashed a couple of months before, and he still hadn't replaced it because he'd always found a better use for the money.

Helen had interrupted him from reading an e-mailed invitation to a poker party sent by one of his old buddies at the television station where he'd worked as a news cameraman until the previous fall. He fingered the card Helen had handed him—Isabel's calling card, and admired the rich texture of the stock and the simple elegance of the design. Both reflected the socialite herself, he thought, tamping down his initial physical reaction and flicking the card straight into the nearest waste container.

"What? You're really not going to get in touch with her?" demanded Helen Rhodes, a blond knock-out and former baby-corporate Web Mistress who owned the cybercafé.

"Nope."

Narrowing her green gaze on him made the small mole at the corner of her right eye all but disappear. "Aren't you curious about what she wants?"

Nick thought about it for a moment and lied. "Nope."

"But it must be important—she's called every day that you've been gone."

He'd been gone away for more than a week this time. So Isabel was persistent in addition to being elegant, smart and a bitch on wheels.

"I'm just not interested in whatever is on the mind of a poor little rich girl," he said.

"Well, I am!"

"That's because you want to run everyone else's lives."

"At least I have one. I don't go underground and disappear on my friends for days or even weeks at a time," Helen stated, her irritation with him finally surfacing. "Where were you when Annie needed us?"

Thinking of their friend's troubles, which had escalated while he'd been gone, Nick flushed guiltily. "It couldn't be helped. Annie's fine now. Better than fine. She's found the one man for her. Or don't you agree?"

The man being Nate Bishop, owner of Cornerstone Realty and the commercial building where all three of them had their businesses. Helen had been suspicious of their landlord from the first when he'd come on to Annie wearing full leathers and riding a Harley, a one-eighty from his business persona. But Nick had known about Nate's intentions all along—had given the guy some pointers with Annie, actually—and now was glad he had no cause for regrets. That Annie was finally getting a man worthy of her brought a smile to Nick's lips.

"Nate really did turn out to be Superman," Helen admitted. "I was wrong."

"That's a first—your admitting it, that is."

Helen gave him one of her deadliest looks and then turned her gaze away. She eyed the waste container as if she were going to climb inside and retrieve the card.

"Go ahead. Do it," Nick said. "I'm sure Isabel would love to spill to you."

"I would love to spill something *on* you."

Nick laughed. "Another empty threat."

Narrowing her gaze on him once more, Helen picked up his water glass and stared at him for one unsettling moment before downing the contents.

"A reprieve," he said.

"Go on, get out of here before I change my mind, before I do something really radical like revoke your caffeine and Internet privileges forever."

"Oh, no, anything but that," Nick said, logging off the Internet as he rose. He'd already taken care of a few business inquiries, and the rest of the e-mail could wait. "Later."

"Yeah, no matter what you do to prevent it, bad pennies always come back."

Nick laughed. He and Helen had given each other

a hard time since they'd met on their first day of college. Now here it was a decade later, and they hadn't grown out of the habit. They also hadn't lost their affection for each other. And for Annie Wilder. The three of them had remained best friends and a strong support system for one another. Together, they had all quit their lucrative rat-race jobs and had put all their savings into businesses they cared about. Unfortunately, his business had been more expensive to finance and harder to get going than an Internet café or lingerie boutique.

He exited the café, which faced the six-corner intersection where Bucktown and Wicker Park met in an eclectic fusion of mind-sets.

The neighborhood held its appeal for artistic types. The streets were dotted with galleries, and the triangular Flatiron Building across the way was taken up by studios of various sorts. It was too early, though, for the pierced and tattooed who frequented the area to be out and about. Instead, the street was filled with commuters—nine-to-five conservative suits and skirts heading for the rapid-transit station down the block. The neighborhood was so eclectic that if he stood in one place long enough, Nick knew every ilk of Chicagoan would eventually pass by.

Nick went with the flow of foot traffic to a nearby doorway that led to the upper floors of the building. He rushed up the flight of stairs to his business—and home, albeit the building was zoned commercial only—situated over Annie's Attic, lingerie store extraordinaire.

But he wasn't alone on the staircase. A woman was

coming down toward him. One with luscious long legs, a graceful demeanor and a familiar face, one even more lovely than he remembered. She had the same good bone structure, the same flawless skin, the same perfect features, but at the moment the delicate flesh around her luminous blue eyes was drawn and tight, making her seem decidedly unhappy.

Nick's smile faded.

Isabel Grayson had shattered him emotionally once.

What the hell made her think he was going to give her a chance to do so again?

ISABEL STOPPED AND STARED at the man coming up the steps toward her and, despite the rush of adrenaline that flowed through her like a raging locomotive, tried to force herself into a state of cool objectivity.

He was tall, maybe six-two now with broad shoulders and great abs—his perfect torso showed through the thin T-shirt, one with the words Film Addict, What's Your Vice? in neat script across one shoulder. His body had changed, certainly, and for the better, but the hair, brown with gold streaks, and the hazel eyes with hidden depths, those she recognized.

A moment's recognition flicked through those familiar eyes, as well…and then it was gone.

Whatever he was thinking was hidden by an expression as impersonal and as neutral as her own. She wondered if his internal reaction to her unexpected presence went as deep as hers. She could barely breathe. He continued up the stairs, looking past her, ignoring her as if she weren't even there. His shoulder brushed against hers, leaving her shaken, trembling inside, but he continued right on by.

"Nick?" she called after him, and to her embarrassment, she sounded a bit breathless saying his name. "You *are* Nicholas Novak, right?" As if she wouldn't recognize the first guy she'd slept with.

"What of it?" He continued upward.

"I've been trying to find you for a week." She turned around and followed him back up to the landing, where he pulled keys from his jeans. Her eyes were level with his butt, as tight and muscular as the rest of him, but she averted her gaze and continued talking to the center of his back, as if there never had been anything between them. "I left my card for you. Isabel Grayson."

He opened the door and turned to face her. "I know who you are, Isabel. I threw the card away."

Anguish swept through her, but she buried it immediately. She was a Grayson, which meant she had steel for a spine. Her mission here *would* be a success. She could negotiate anything.

"May I come in?"

"I have work to do."

He hadn't changed, she thought. The rudest teenager in their high school had grown into an even ruder man.

"Please. This is important."

He sighed and threw up his hands. "All right." Though he turned his back on her and went inside, he left the door open. "Come in and make it quick."

Isabel didn't give him a chance to change his mind. She entered and closed the door, whose window bore the gold-stenciled words, Nick's Knack, Videography, to identify the business.

The high-ceilinged, multiwindowed room was a studio of sorts. A backdrop graced one wall. Several lights hung from a ceiling grid. And one end of the studio was filled with racks of equipment. For editing, she supposed.

At the other end, in a corner, she spotted a trundle bed, covers strewn across it as if he'd slept there. And a shelf of free weights lined the wall nearby.

"So what is so important, Isabel, that you hound me for an entire week?"

She brought her attention back to the man who was now a stranger to her. "My sister Louise. *She's* that important."

"So what about her?"

He'd never met Louise, so it was understandable that he might not remember her. Isabel doubted he kept up with politics or politicians. And even if he did, she doubted Senator William Grayson was on his list of people to watch.

"Louise is missing."

He digested that for a moment, then said, "Maybe she simply wanted to get away from the Graysons."

He sounded as if he'd had experience in that department. No secret to her why, either, Isabel thought. Hopefully he wouldn't hold against her what had happened between them so many years before.

"She's only seventeen."

"Eleven years younger than you."

Startled that he should remember exactly how old

she was, Isabel murmured, "She was Mother's late-life gift."

Actually, Mother had once callously called Louise her afterthought, but that was only because of how angry she'd been with the teenager, Isabel assured herself. Louise had always been a handful. A spitfire like himself, her father had once proclaimed proudly, going on to mutter something about having another politician in the making.

Not that he felt proud of her any longer.

"If your sister is missing," Nick now said, a shadow of concern flitting through his otherwise mulish expression, "it's a matter for the police."

"She's not missing as in being a victim. She's a runaway and she's seventeen and just graduated from high school. I'm told this isn't anything unusual. That teenagers hit the streets every day and that if she doesn't want to be found, she probably won't be." Isabel took a steadying breath and slowed down. "Louise is a few months away from being an adult and adults are allowed to disappear if they want to. The police aren't going to put on a manhunt for her. She'll just be another name in a database."

"But with your father's influence…"

"Yes, you would think so, wouldn't you? But that would mean he would actually have to make a fuss. He would have to ask for special treatment for a member of his family." Controlling her anger so that her voice was even, she added, "He would have to put himself in the spotlight when it wouldn't be to his advantage."

Nick's eyebrows shot up. "I see."

He didn't see, she thought, not really. Nor did she. She didn't know how her father could continue to skirt around the truth when a member of his family was in trouble. But she would think about it later. For now, finding her sister, making certain she was safe, had to be her focus.

"So why come to *me?*" Nick asked.

"Your name came up as someone who knows the kids on the streets. I was told you're doing a documentary on runaways. If that's true, you might be able to find her."

"An assumption that's questionable at best."

"You're my only hope."

Nick shook his head. "Then don't get your hopes up, because I have neither the time nor the interest to get involved in your problems. Besides, I have a bond with these kids. I don't betray any trusts they ask me to keep."

"You wouldn't have to," she promised.

"Hire a private investigator. Hell, Isabel, with your money, you can hire a whole firm."

Isabel's insides twisted at his words. This was going to be more difficult than she'd hoped. She had to admit a part of her motivation in seeking him out was curiosity about Nick himself. Or maybe she just wanted to get him out of her head once and for all... though that didn't seem likely. Even now, even when she had more important things on her mind, Isabel couldn't help remembering how his touch had made her melt...and wondering what it would be like today.

Louise was the priority here, and instinct told Isabel

that Nick was her best bet at finding her sister without the situation being leaked to the press. She wasn't about to give up.

"Maybe if I told you something about my little sister?"

"Go ahead." Nick made himself comfortable in a portable canvas-and-tubing chair, the kind people brought to outdoor concerts. "But you're wasting your time."

He indicated she should sit in the mate to his chair, but too nervous, she shook her head and paced instead. She feared if she got that close to him, she just might come completely unglued.

"Louise is a bright kid—"

"As would be expected of a Grayson."

"—and a little wild—"

"Which wouldn't be."

"May I speak without the editorial?"

"I thought you were used to that, your father being who he is and all."

Isabel gritted her teeth. She needed Nick Novak's help, would do anything to enlist his cooperation. And unless she made nice, she wasn't going to get it.

"Louise and I have always been very close. She always came to me, to talk, to get advice. She was levelheaded, thought things through before acting. Then something changed several months ago. She got into some trouble," Isabel admitted, remembering how her sister had started acting up. "More than once, in fact. Nothing serious, but it was out of character and enough to bring Dad's wrath down on her."

"Because she wasn't displaying the proper behavior? Oh, sorry. No editorializing. I keep forgetting."

He hadn't forgotten anything, Isabel decided, no more than she had. Was he really thinking only about her father's interference in their lives or was he thinking about them? About how they'd fallen in love? About how they'd consummated their feelings for each other?

Staring into his familiar hazel eyes, she couldn't help but remember the past herself. Her heart beat a little harder, her pulse rushed faster, as she considered the possibilities. Licking her lips, Isabel forced her mind where it needed to be. On her sister.

"She's been trying to get Dad's attention, unfortunately in the wrong way, making up excuses for her actions afterward. All she did was make him furious with her. They fought...horribly—" about what, she hoped Nick wouldn't ask at the moment "—and then she disappeared. We thought she'd gone to a friend's house and was trying to make a point. But I've checked with her friends and none of them have admitted seeing her. And then her best friend, Rosalyn, got scared and admitted that Louise stopped by several days ago and told her she was never coming home again."

"So why no big police hunt?" Nick asked again. "Why no private investigators? *You* make a fuss if your father won't."

Her doing so would be the end of everything, Isabel thought, and yet, if push came to shove, she would do what she had to. Only not now. Not when there was a possibility that Nick could help her.

"That wouldn't be appropriate at the moment," she said simply.

"So you still jump to your father's tune."

Heat seared her neck, making Isabel want to shake the man until he agreed to help her. But all she would shake was his complacency, not his conscience. In the past Nick had tended to let things slide unless he got really angry. Then you didn't want to be on his bad side. But his good side made up for those other times. At least it *had*. She really didn't know him anymore.

That's why she wasn't about to tell him everything. Not yet. Not until she was sure of him.

"My father is making a certain amount of sense this time." Not an outright lie. She didn't want to deceive Nick, but she was desperate to get to her sister before Louise came to harm. "He thinks Louise is trying to worry us and he has more important things that need his attention."

"More important than his own daughter who is out on the streets?"

To his credit, Nick sounded appalled.

Isabel swallowed hard. Senator William Grayson, respected politician, had used his family to launch his career, and once he'd been off and running…well, she and Louise had been put on the back burner, to be taken out and used as needed, just as had their mother, Natalie. She wondered if things would have been different if she and Louise had been born male. Her father had always mourned the lack of a son to follow in his footsteps…as if she couldn't have.

As it was, Isabel had spent a lifetime doing things her father wanted to gain his approval, just as Louise had acted up to get his attention. Other than being a model wife when necessary, their mother had always made her own way, her own life, not seeming to care that her husband the senator neglected her.

Isabel only wondered if, after she resolved this newest crisis, she would have the courage to do the same and walk away from her father's influence once and for all.

"Maybe the good senator doesn't want the spotlight shining his way when there's something negative for the public to see?" Nick speculated.

Isabel's heart skipped a beat. He always had been intuitive. But she wasn't about to admit to anything, not yet, not until she was sure she had his loyalty.

"My father is very careful about his reputation."

Isabel stopped mere inches from Nick. Not even touching him, she squeezed her thighs together to chase away her spontaneous response to his heat. She imagined it oozed from him in waves. She wasn't immune to him, not even after all these years. Now she knew she wasn't going to be able to put him and the past behind her so easily.

But what was she going to do about it?

Licking her lips, she said, "I don't want a private investigator, Nick. I want *you*." Horrified by her lack of will, she realized that she really did, in the most physical sense. "So will you do it? For me?"

NICK SMOTHERED A LAUGH and noted how quickly Isabel flushed and backed off.

Isabel Grayson didn't want him and never had. She'd toyed with him—a "have" getting her jollies by stringing along a "have-not." She'd probably been the richest girl in their high school and he'd been the poorest boy, for sure. But now the rules had changed. She wanted something from him and he wanted nothing to do with her. Now that the shoe was on the other foot, so to speak, he couldn't help but wonder how that made her feel.

"Did you really think that would work?" he asked.

"Work?"

"Your coming on to me."

She blinked and her expression changed. "*Would* that work?"

For a moment Nick was flabbergasted. Was she really willing to do anything to get him to agree?

The idea that he could have her in his bed set his imagination to work. He eyed the narrow trundle bed, thought about taking her right there, having her beg him for more. His growing erection throbbed as he turned his attention to her body, so much fuller, more tempting than it had been as a teenager. He imagined slipping his hand up the inside of her leg—her suit skirt was short enough—and teasing her until she begged him to plunge his fingers into her wetness, just as she used to all those years ago.

For a moment, he was tempted to see how far he could go, if he could actually get to her, but Nick knew Isabel didn't mean it any more than she had meant anything she'd said to him when he'd been in her thrall. She was a Grayson, a political animal, and he had to remember that. She would do anything, say anything, to get what she wanted.

Only when the time came for payout...well, then, no doubt, she would change her story.

"How's business?" Isabel suddenly asked.

Startled by the abrupt change in subject, Nick said, "Excuse me?"

"No one seems to have an address for you other than this one." Isabel looked around the studio, her gaze stopping at the rumpled trundle bed. "No apartment, which suggests you might be short of money." She turned back to him and her expression told him she thought she was in control once more. "I'm not short of money, Nick, as you noted earlier. So how much?"

His gut tightened. She was trying to buy him with money—the thing that had stood between them when they were teenagers.

Nothing had changed.

"I don't want your money."

"Then what do you want? Work? I can get you work."

"Your father's next campaign?" he asked, knowing what the answer would be. "Can you guarantee that I can produce his commercials?"

Now *that* would be payback worth savoring, but only if he got it in writing.

"I—I don't have control over Dad. But I have other contacts and I can see what I can do."

"Not interested."

The only thing he was interested in was seeing how far she was willing to go to get what she wanted, Nick thought, his gaze brushing the full breasts that couldn't be hidden by a business suit. It would be an intellectual exercise only, of course, he thought as he steeled himself against an instantaneous reaction to her.

"What else do you want?" she asked, her voice suddenly hollow. "Name it."

He wanted her. Here. Now. Hell, anytime. Maybe then he would be able to get her out of his system.

That she'd broken his heart, had left him with nothing inside, didn't seem to matter. She'd driven him away and into the worst year of his life, a year of hopelessness, a year in which he'd done things he wasn't proud of to survive.

Isabel didn't know that, of course, and why would she care unless she got a taste of it herself?

Or would she even care then? he wondered, a flash of brilliance hitting him. He knew exactly how to get rid of her.

An ironic smile curling his lips, Nick said, "You would never go for it, Isabel. If I were to look for your sister—and I say that with great reservations— you would have to come with me."

"Of course, I would expect to."

Isabel suddenly came alive, relief making her shine, giving him a glimpse of the girl she used to be. Rather, the girl he'd thought she'd been.

She went on. "I've been looking for Louise myself since she left home. I've even driven through this neighborhood—her friend Rosalyn lives in Wicker Park and Louise has spent a lot of time around here, including that visit the other day—"

"Whoa, I don't think you have the big picture here, Isabel. When I say look, I mean from the inside."

"I don't understand."

"The streets, Isabel. You'll have to give up your cushy home and your nice clothes and your meals in fine restaurants. You'll have to accompany me along the dangerous city streets of Chicago like a runaway, panhandling and sleeping in hovels who knows where."

And for a moment, one foolish moment, Nick hoped she would agree to his terms.

"What?" She seemed shocked. "Why?"

"You want to find someone living on the streets, you walk in their shoes."

The color drained from her face. "You think Louise is living on the streets?"

"Where else? Hotels don't open their doors to runaways, unless she's using Daddy's credit card."

"Louise has her own credit card, but she's not using it. I checked."

"Smart girl. She doesn't want you to find her."

"But there are other places...something!"

"And you haven't exhausted them?"

"The ones I know about or was told about, yes. I went to a couple of shelters, but they say the kids they take are with parents."

Nick nodded. "There are only a few shelters in the metropolitan area that take in homeless teens and those are funded privately. So runaways don't normally go to shelters."

"Dear God, then how do they survive?"

"Any way they can, Isabel. Begging...conning... prostituting themselves."

Finally the magnitude of her sister's situation

seemed to hit her. White as a sheet and shaky, to boot, Isabel took the chair he'd offered her a moment ago.

"Oh, Louise, Louise," she murmured, and the sound was so heart-wrenching that Nick almost gave way and agreed to find the girl himself.

No! He wouldn't do it. Wouldn't put himself through that hell again. What was he thinking? Isabel Grayson was poison to him. She'd nearly ruined him. He had to keep that uppermost in his mind.

"I think we're done here," he said, rising to escort her to the door.

"No, we're not. You made me an offer—"

"I said *if*," he reminded her. "And that's a big if."

"I'll come with you," she whispered. "I'll live on the streets. I'll do whatever I have to, to find my sister."

Nick steeled himself to the desperation in her voice. He understood desperation, had lived with it for years. He understood the streets, too. Understood they could be death to kids. Not that most didn't survive somehow. But the streets changed them. Hardened them. Made them look at everything around them with suspicion. He felt sorry for Louise, even if she was a Grayson.

More important, Nick reminded himself, he knew Isabel. He'd hoped never to see her again…had hated her for a while…but had never been able to get her out of his system. Now here she was, big as life, more beautiful and tempting than ever, begging for his help.

But she could afford to buy help, another part of him argued. She'd simply refused because her father wanted things done discreetly. Well, the hell with what Senator William Grayson wanted. *This* time, the ball wasn't in Grayson's court. The senator wasn't going to pull the strings in Nick Novak's life!

"Hire a private investigator," Nick said again, knowing Isabel could be his undoing and that he would be crazy to risk himself again.

"No, please, Nick," Isabel pleaded, rising to face him. "Help me and I'll do anything you say."

Her classic features were flushed and open and a strand of pale blond hair dared to stray out of place over her cheek, begging to be tucked back behind her ear. Staring at her, Nick felt himself tighten. Beneath that elegant beauty, Isabel Grayson still smoldered. He could practically smell the telltale musk signaling to a man that a woman was in heat.

God help him, she was still the biggest temptation he'd ever tried to resist, and he craved her more than anything. Though they'd only spent that one night together in complete abandon, she had ruined him for other women. He'd spent years comparing, wondering what she would be like now....

He *was* a fool!

Despite the fact he wanted in the worst way to turn his back on her, he wanted Isabel even more. If only it could be on his terms this time.

But he knew it wouldn't happen.

Even so, the words came out of his mouth before he could stop them. "The nights get lonely on the streets, Isabel." He moved closer, a threat to her neat and pretty life. "I don't like being lonely." He hooked that stray silver-blond strand with a finger and remembered what it had been like to run both hands through her hair when she'd worn it loose down her back. "You want me to find your sister?"

"Yes, please."

He stepped even closer so his breath feathered her face. She shivered in response but didn't give way. He felt himself weaken. An internal battle ensued about whether or not he should cave. Unless he did something fast, something to make her turn tail and run, he would be lost.

"Fine," he murmured seductively. "Then you not only keep me company, you keep me warm at night. Deal?"

That should do it. Now she would look at him with contempt and storm out that door.

Isabel's momentarily shocked expression faded, leaving one that was neutral and indicative of a woman in control.

Her full lips parted slightly, and she licked them before saying, "Deal."

2

HE'D BEEN HAD.

That was the first thought that crossed Nick's mind as he registered Isabel's too easy agreement.

She appeared too confident, too controlled. She probably figured he would somehow find Louise right off the bat and then she wouldn't have to come through with her part of the bargain.

Irritatingly, he was far too eager for her to meet his challenge to keep him warm at night.

Crossing his arms over his chest, he said, "I don't believe you."

"Don't believe what?" she asked. "That I care enough about my sister to do whatever it takes to find her? Or is it that you question *my* ethics?"

The way she said *my* made him think she questioned *his*. Understandable. Isabel believed he'd been serious about the deal. She had no way of knowing he'd been looking for a way out.

Moving away from him and examining his camcorder, she murmured, "So...runaways...why choose that subject for your documentary?"

"I think it's a growing problem in too many dysfunctional families."

"And you think that *you* can find a solution?"

"That's not my job."

"Then what is your job?"

"To turn my lens on a specific aspect of society and make people think about it."

"You want your audience to think about runaways. And then what?"

"In the best-case scenario, do something."

"Like what?"

"Like help one kid on the street," he said. "Or better yet, learn to recognize the warning signs and do whatever it takes to stop a kid from running before it happens."

Isabel stopped cold and glared at him. "Are you telling me I should have known Louise was about to run?"

He shrugged. "I didn't say that."

"I don't know how anyone could say for certain what's in another person's mind."

"All depends on how you approach it."

"How do *you* approach it? I mean, how do you get information out of people?"

"I approach it without judgment," he said. "I simply turn the camera on the kids and they spill."

"Spill?"

"Their guts."

"That easy? You just put the camera on a kid and he gives you his life's story?"

"Well, not always, but there have been moments. Why not let me show you?"

"Sure, I'd like to see some of your documentary footage."

"I was thinking more in terms of a live demo," he said.

Nick took Isabel by the arm and swept her back toward the camera and the stool that he'd placed before it. "Sit."

"And what?"

"Talk."

"Me? About what?"

Rather than answering directly, he indicated that she should take the seat. Seeming reluctant only for a moment, she did. Then he flipped on the grid lights that gave her face and hair dimension, and he checked the viewer. He zoomed in tight on her features. On her lips. Full, tempting lips.

He remembered their taste, their feel on his tongue.

Gut tightening, Nick zoomed out to a medium shot from the waist up, hit the record button and stood back so that, looking through the lights that shone on her, Isabel wouldn't be able to see him clearly in the shadowed area behind the camera.

"So what's the object of this game?" she asked, seeming in control once more.

"Tell me about yourself."

She blinked, then said, "Isabel Grayson...twenty-eight...single...majored in political science...work as a press liaison for my father, Senator William Grayson."

"Tell me about yourself," Nick repeated, wanting to hear about her, not about her father.

She seemed confused for a second before starting again. "I'm smart...determined...loyal."

"Tell me about yourself," he said for a third time, wishing for some insight to the real woman.

Exasperation replaced confusion as she demanded, "What is it you want from me?"

A loaded question if ever he'd heard one. He wanted everything she had to give. He wanted her in his bed, where he would make up new ways to take her. But he wasn't about to go there, not now. And if he were smart, he would never go there, he thought, suddenly realizing that she still had the power to affect him, maybe even destroy the part of him that had never fully recovered.

So what he said was "Something you're not giving me." Honesty was what he wanted.

"Obviously, but what?"

"Tell me one thing that no one knows about you." Something that would tell him there was more to her than he feared, something that would help him figure her out.

Frowning now, she asked, "Why would I?"

"Because you want to play the game."

"Well, maybe I don't, really," Isabel admitted, sliding off the stool.

His "Aha!" caught her where she stood. "You don't really care if I help you find Louise or not."

"That's not true! Of course I do!" Clearly uncomfortable, she sat back down. "What was the question again?"

"Tell me something about yourself that no one else knows."

Her control had slipped. He sensed it. He saw it.

He heard it in her voice when she finally said, "I...I don't always like myself."

Who did? Nick wondered, surprised that she'd admitted it. "Because..."

"Sometimes I do a thing—not because I believe in it, but because it's expedient."

The hallmark of a true politician, he thought. And yet her admitting it made him respect her. "How does that make you feel?"

"I try not to think about it too closely."

Nick sensed the depth of her sudden discomfort and thought of a possible way out for himself. It wasn't too late to make Isabel change her mind. He should never have played along with her from the start. But since he had, he now had to see it through.

"Am I expedient?" he suddenly asked, facing what he feared to be true. "Is that why you came to me for help?"

Heightened color flushed her face. "Yes, I suppose you could think of it that way."

"What other way is there?"

Isabel looked away from the camera and away from him. Though she might be doing her damnedest to keep the experiment under her own control, Nick was an expert in getting information out of reluctant subjects. And if it was too late to get himself out of this predicament, if he was going to put himself on the line for her, then at least he needed to know that she could learn something from the experience.

He stepped forward into the light and caught her immediate attention.

"So what is it you're trying to hide, Isabel?"

"Nothing." Her mouth tightened.

He moved closer. "What else would you do to find Louise, to make sure she's safe?"

"Whatever it takes."

"Why?"

"Because she's my sister and I love her and it's up to me to watch out for her!"

Damn! Her obvious love and worry for her kid sister got to him like nothing else could. Nick didn't state the obvious. The depth of responsibility that she was talking about was that of a parent, not a sibling. Neglect of his children when they weren't expedient to him—Nick believed that of the senator. But what about Mrs. Grayson?

Suddenly Nick caught himself. What the hell was he doing, working up sympathy for Isabel Grayson and her problems? He wanted nothing to do with her or her family, he reminded himself. Not again. The object was to get her to default.

Or was it?

She's in your system, and isn't it time you got her out? a little voice argued.

Too dangerous. Don't do it! another part of him responded. Knowing Isabel, she wouldn't leave it be just because he said no. Letting it go had to be her idea.

Suddenly desperate to make her call it quits, Nick advanced on her—close enough that her familiar scent set his senses on edge—and said, "So, you *say* you would do anything. Prove it."

"Wh-what? How?"

"Use your imagination," he said silkily, liking the

way his low intonation made her eyes grow wide. "We're going to be working closely together. On the streets. Just you and me. And the *nights*..." He let his voice linger on the last. "Are you prepared for the *nights,* Isabel?"

Apparently, she wasn't. He swore he could smell fear emanating from her in increasing waves. He was behind her now, staring at the back of her long, elegant neck, fighting a sudden, powerful urge to taste the delicate skin at the nape. He remembered what she tasted like, remembered how easily she responded to him.

But he didn't need that disrupting his life.

Unclenching his jaw, he leaned over slightly and whispered directly in her ear, "So show me what you've got."

She shuddered.

That should do it, he thought. Now Isabel would call a halt to this madness.

Only, she wasn't doing any such thing. Still stiff, she took in an audible breath and lifted hands that shook slightly to the top button of her blouse. Watching over her shoulder, he could see every minute movement. Fascinated, he couldn't avert his eyes. Couldn't tell her to stop.

How far was she willing to go?

"What is it you want from me, Nick?" she asked, her voice calm, steely even, as she undid the first button. "Proof that I'll keep you warm at night? Fine." A second button released its hold on the material. "I can do that. And I'll be whatever, whoever you want me to be."

Staring down into the cleavage opening up to him, Nick told himself that he wanted her gone.

Liar!

His body told him what a liar he was as she finished unbuttoning her blouse with the finesse of a professional. From his vantage point, he was staring straight down at nicely shaped breasts that spilled from a flesh-colored material so see-through that she might as well have not been wearing anything at all.

His heart pumped faster. His mouth went drier. His erection grew harder.

Determined to push her to the edge from which she would finally flee, he pressed his length into her back and was gut-shot when she arched against him. He could see her nipples flush and pebble through the see-through material. The obvious offer was too tempting. He couldn't help himself. Slipping his hands around the back of her neck, he circled her throat and then slowly glided his fingers lower, along the trail between her breasts.

A small gasp escaped her and Nick flushed so hot he felt burned.

Arching higher so that her breasts practically begged to be fondled, she slid her hands around the back of his thighs and pulled him tighter so that the length of his erection lay against her soft buttocks.

She moved so slightly that he might have imagined it. Except that she moved again and again—small, furtive movements—until he was ready to come. Her breasts slipped into his palms as if of their own volition. He thumbed her already-aroused nipples through the thin material and she moaned softly.

His mouth ached to surround her breasts with his wet heat; his cock ached to be surrounded by hers.

And if her fingers tightening on the backs of his thighs were any indication, they were of a single mind, Nick realized, as Isabel moaned more deeply, her sexual response to him triggering long-repressed memories.

They'd been young then, and innocent. And they'd shared their bodies with an openness he'd never experienced since.

The vivid recollections were overpowering, too potent for comfort. Forcing his hands from her tempting flesh, Nick moved away, staying behind her to regain his composure.

But she swung around on the stool in a challenge.

"Well?" she asked coolly, the impassioned woman of a moment ago gone. Just a trace of lust and maybe something else, something deeper, remained in her eyes. "Did I pass your test, Nick? Will I do?"

A moment ago, he would have sworn she was as turned on as he. He still swore it even though her expression remained passive and her gaze went purposely blank. She was looking straight at him as expectantly as if they were making a business deal.

Isabel *had* been turned on, he knew it. But her heart hadn't been in it—which was good, Nick told himself, because his heart couldn't be involved again, either.

Finally, he answered, "Perfect."

HAVING PASSED HIS STUPID TEST, Isabel swallowed hard and tamped down her emotions. She could play poker with the best of them, and they would never know when they were about to be beaten. And the best of them by far and large were reporters and politicians, people she dealt with on a day-to-day basis on her father's behalf.

By comparison, Nick Novak would be a piece of cake.

She didn't want to dwell on how affected she had been by the heated encounter. She'd known being near Nick was going to be a challenge. She just hadn't known how devastating he could still be to her. Her easy response to him was something of a shock.

"So it's a deal, then," she said, far more calmly than she was feeling.

What had she gotten herself into?

Isabel held her hand out for a businesslike shake and steeled herself for the emotions that roiled through her when Nick took her hand. He let it go quickly, as if touching her bothered him, too. What would it be like keeping him warm at night? Could they possibly recapture anything of the past? she wondered, remembering how loved and safe she'd felt when he'd held her in his arms after making love to her. Or would she just be a convenience to him?

"So, how do we proceed?" she asked, feeling anything but businesslike inside.

Not that she would let Nick know how she was feeling. Maybe in his mind, she had a little humiliation coming. Maybe he planned a little delayed revenge because of the way she'd broken it off with him.

"We'll start tonight."

"Tonight." A pulse ticked in her throat. He was

stalling, holding out for what he could get from her before they found Louise. "Why wait?"

"Because I have an appointment with a client this afternoon, a potential industrial video for me to shoot. And then tomorrow I was supposed to get together with Gideon over at Club Undercover to plan some new dance videos he wants for the club, so I'll have to set a new appointment with him. I do run a business, you know. Besides, night is when we can most easily find the kids."

"Oh." She nodded. "Tonight, then. Shall I meet you here?"

"Downstairs at Helen's Cybercafé at eight."

Nodding, she passed him and headed for the door.

"Isabel, wait."

Isabel stopped short, one hand on the doorknob. She would not let him see how she was feeling. She would not!

Turning back to face Nick, she was caught by something in his gaze. Quickly glancing away, she stared back at his equipment and realized the red light on the camera was still glowing. Meaning the equipment was still recording.

He said, "About tonight…go home and change into something a little more…casual."

Had he actually thought she planned on hitting the streets in clothes that would make her a target? "I'm not stupid."

"I didn't think you were." He studied her thoroughly, from the tips of her Italian shoes to her carefully coiffed hair. "But you'll have to go some to fit in."

She remembered when *he* was the one who hadn't fit in. "Don't worry, Nick. I'll be appropriate...just as I always am."

Agreeing to the deal at all was hard enough on her self-respect that he should be satisfied. Only desperation for Louise would allow her to do something so...so...so crass. Only a man like Nick Novak would expect it of her, score to settle or not.

"By the way," he said as she gripped the door handle, "where is home these days?"

"I'm still in the DePaul area." Figuring she knew what he was thinking, she flushed and met his gaze. "Yes, Nick, I still live at home, if that's all right with you." She'd had to stay there for Louise's sake.

"Hey, it's your life."

Leaving the close quarters of Nick's place relieved a huge measure of tension. Isabel felt as if she were taking her first breath since running into Nick on the staircase.

Tonight would be easier, she told herself. They would be surrounded by people, searching for her sister. She could get through that, no problem.

But what about afterward? How would she handle spending the night with him?

A shiver of dread shimmied up her spine as Isabel tried to push from her mind what Nick would expect of her. Of the clever things that she would have to do to keep him satisfied. But the sensual images that came to her wouldn't be easily banished. Nor would the tension that had built up again from the inside out. Wanting him was like a sickness.

Try as she might, she'd never been able to forget

Nick. But he wasn't the same boy she'd fallen in love with, and maybe being with him now would cure her.

Hailing a taxi, she headed straight for her father's Chicago office in the Lincoln Park West neighborhood. Since Congress was in summer recess, he was in town but chafing to get on with business in other parts of the state. Anything rather than deal with his own daughter, Isabel thought. William Grayson's career had always come first.

Take the money he'd put into his office. While a politician normally rented an accessible storefront office in the home state, not her father. With private funds, he'd bought one of the remaining three-flat greystones on Clark Street. The tenants of the apartments on the upper two floors supposedly paid the mortgage and building expenses, and her father had turned the entire first floor into a luxurious office suite.

Isabel shared an office with Boyd Cummings, the other press assistant. Boyd spent more time in D.C. with her father when Congress was in session, while she handled things here at the home front. Boyd was a golden boy with fair good looks and unusual sea-blue eyes that set many a female heart aflame, both here and in D.C.

Despite that he was a decent guy, she herself had never felt any attraction to the man, maybe because she wasn't fond of playboy types but probably just because he had her father's stamp of approval. She'd dated too many of those men who'd been more interested in her father's work than in her to be intrigued by Boyd. Both her professional and personal world was populated with mostly politicians and reporters, so she had a hard time meeting anyone who actually interested her.

Except for Nick Novak...

Not that she didn't like Boyd, she thought, shoving Nick to the back of her mind. But she saw him as a supportive friend, sort of like the brother she'd never had.

"So, heard anything about the kid?" Boyd asked as she settled herself in to look over the mound of mail on her desk.

The kid referred to Louise, of course. The two seemed fond of each other, and Isabel had long suspected that Louise had grown into young womanhood with a crush on Boyd.

"No, but I'm hoping for a break soon," she said, without qualifying the statement.

"Really? I miss the brat, and I'm worried about her," Boyd admitted. "If we don't get a break on her whereabouts soon, the senator will have to change his tune and let the authorities in on the matter."

"I don't think it'll come to that."

Isabel didn't want to go into it further, not with a colleague.

She hadn't even gone into it with Nora Hamilton, her college roommate and longtime best friend. Isabel now fought the urge to call, knowing Nora had problems of her own. Man problems, as usual.

Which made her think of Nick again. He was a problem, all right, in every sense of the word. But she would get through this somehow.

Isabel got to the growing pile of work on her desk,

but she couldn't concentrate. She kept thinking about Nick, about what she was going to have to do to keep him looking for Louise.

Finally giving up on routine work, she glanced at her watch. Just enough time that her father would still be in. Traditionally, he took lunch at one o'clock or even later, so that any constituents who wanted to see him during their own lunch hour could.

Isabel made her way to the back of the building and her father's domain, where she knocked at his office door and opened it.

"You have nothing to worry about," her father was saying in a low tone as she slipped inside, gently closing the door behind her. He was sitting, his broad, physically fit body turned away from her, and staring out a window. Sounding exasperated, he said, "How the hell many times do I have to reassure you!"

Isabel wondered what kind of problem they were facing now. Thinking she didn't need to be putting out any more fires, she sighed, which signaled to her father that he wasn't alone.

Voice smoothing out to cordial, he said, "I'll have to get back to you on that one."

The moment he hung up, she said, "I hope that's something Boyd can fix because—"

"It's something *I'll* fix!" he said sharply. His eyes, a shade darker than his silver hair, narrowed on her.

Isabel raised her eyebrows but didn't comment. "I just stopped in to let you know I'm going to be out looking for Louise. I've gotten nowhere alone, so I've brought in reinforcements."

"The hell you say—I told you, no police!"

He was certainly in a mood, Isabel thought. "No police," she reassured him.

"Or private investigators. I don't need some damn gumshoe blackmailing me to keep my secrets."

His secrets. Yes, that is what had gotten them into this fix, something she hadn't told Nick.

"No private investigator," she assured him. "I'm calling out a favor from Nick Novak."

Her father cursed until his face turned beet red. "I told you about him!"

"I'm not sixteen anymore. And I...*we* need him to find Louise. Nick knows kids on the street. He's been doing a documentary on them. They trust him. They'll talk to him."

"And *he'll* talk to the press."

Isabel shook her head. "He won't, because I'll see to it."

Just as she saw to everything else her father needed. But, more and more, she was becoming torn about her loyalty to him, in this case more than ever. She had a lot to think about. Surely she could find something else to do professionally that would be equally satisfying and a lot less painful.

The door opened behind her and Boyd walked in holding a sheaf of papers. "Sorry, sir, I need your signature."

Her father waved Boyd over. And to Isabel, he said, "All right. How long do you think it will take?"

"I have no idea. I thought I would find Louise right away, or that she would come home." Isabel shook her head. "This is our last shot at finding her quietly."

"I'm sure you'll do whatever it takes." Already signing the papers, her father asked distractedly, "You'll call in every day and touch base with me personally?"

Isabel blinked. That was it? No more argument? No questions? Not even simple curiosity as to how she would keep Nick Novak in line?

No, of course not.

I'm sure you'll do whatever it takes....

Senator William Grayson figured his loyal daughter would clean up his mess before it touched him politically, and that's all he cared about. Even if he knew what she'd agreed to, he would have considered the political expediency of her actions and have slept well that night.

"All right, then," she said, fighting the huge lump in her throat. "I'll be leaving shortly."

Suddenly her father looked to the doorway and waved in his chief of staff, Jeff Enger, a thin man who looked better for his middle age, with silver threading his dark hair. Another politician with big ambitions, he'd lately given her cause to wonder how long he would be loyal to her father before setting off on his own campaign trail.

"I have the results of that poll," Enger said.

"About time." Her father waved Isabel off without so much as a glance.

As she left the office, Boyd caught up to her. "Listen, Isabel, if there's anything I can do to help you find Louise, all you have to do is ask."

If only she could. But Boyd couldn't help her. Only Nick Novak had the wherewithal to get *this* job done.

"I've got it covered, Boyd."

"It's just…you seem so upset. If you want to talk about it, I've got a spare ear," he joked gently.

Isabel gave him a grateful smile. "Thanks, Boyd. I appreciate the concern." At least someone had noticed her unhappiness. She glanced back to her father's office and saw that he was already preoccupied with another phone call. She felt heartsick when she said, "When Louise is home safe, then maybe I'll take you up on that offer." She flashed Boyd a smile. "I have some important decisions to make and I could use a friend."

"Sounds serious."

Turning away from him, she murmured, "You have no idea."

And neither did her father.

3

HAVING RETHOUGHT THE DEAL he'd made with Isabel, Nick entered the cybercafé earlier than usual, using the need to check his e-mail as his excuse to visit Helen.

Not only did he use the Internet to keep up with his buddies from the television station and to check in on a couple of lists of video professionals that he'd joined, but to do actual business, as well. Helen had created a Web page for him that had brought him several new clients over the past six months, including the industrial client he'd met with earlier. The meeting had gone well, and if he could do business on a regular basis with the man's company, it would quickly get him out of his money crunch.

A while later, just as he knew she would after closing up shop, Annie Wilder walked in to share a cup of coffee and the gossip of the day. Annie and Helen chose a table near the windows. Nick barely waited a beat before closing down his e-mail account to join them.

"Looking good," he said approvingly as he slid in across from Annie. She'd edited her waif look to include a swirly skirt and some kind of shiny froufrou thing tied in her long brown hair, little details that made her appear more feminine and prettier than usual. Maybe true love did that, he thought, along with bringing a sparkle to the gray eyes behind her frameless glasses, as well as shading her cheeks with a hint of natural color.

Or was their Annie actually wearing makeup?

Nick gaped at her long enough that Helen said, "Close your mouth before you catch flies."

He patted his stomach. "A little protein wouldn't hurt."

"I'm not feeding you," she warned.

"Did I ask you to?"

"Come home with me and I'll feed you good," Gloria Delgado offered as she stopped at the table. "I know exactly how to satisfy a man's appetites."

The dark-haired Latina in the colorful, too short outfit and too high heels was Annie's employee. Sipping at a coffee, she watched him over the rim of the paper cup, her dark eyes challenging.

"Gloria, I've always thought you were more woman than I could handle," he said with a laugh.

"You won't know for sure until you try me."

Not the first time she'd made that suggestion, Nick thought.

Helen cleared her throat. "Annie, have you ever told Gloria about Nick's marathon weekend?"

Annie grinned. "I don't usually admit to being friends with a man who has women coming and going all hours of the night, one after the other."

"Hmm, sounds *ver-r-ry* interesting," Gloria said, then gave Nick a wide-eyed look. "You might even be able to keep up with *me*."

Annie snorted and Helen threw up her hands in feigned disgust. Nick laughed and the good-humored Gloria did, as well. She loved to flirt and Nick loved that about her. But she was his good friend's employee and, as such, had always been off-limits.

"So what's up, Nick?" Annie asked. "I have the feeling you've got something on your mind."

He gave them an edited version of the plan to find Louise—sans his requirement that Isabel keep him warm at night—in the hope they'd talk him out of it. Of course, he'd ensured that they'd keep the information confidential.

He'd already told Nathaniel Bishop—their landlord and Annie's true love—the *whole* story, dirty details included. Nate had seemed amused and had offered him some practical help rather than giving him an excuse to back out of the deal. In return, Nate had intimated he was working up to pop the question to Annie.

"You're a hero to put yourself out like this for someone you don't even like," Annie said instead.

"I didn't say I didn't like her."

Her eyebrows popped up high above her glasses. "Helen told me you threw away her card and wanted nothing to do with her."

Nick glared at the blonde, who asked, "Why does this Grayson woman think you're this big expert who can find her sister, anyhow?"

"Because of my current video project."

"Doing dance videos for Club Undercover?"

"I've been gathering video interviews of runaways for a documentary." He tapped out a nervous beat on the tabletop. "It's a personal project." One he hadn't told them about and didn't want to get into, at least not yet. Realizing that his friends were looking at him as though he'd grown two extra heads, he asked, "What?"

"Well, at least now we'll have some idea of where you go when you disappear for days or weeks at a time," Helen commented.

Annie added, "And if you ever want to talk about it—the personal project or why you're doing it—feel free."

"And feel free to ask for help if you need it," Gloria said. "Don't be like this one." She waved a beringed finger with a long chartreuse nail at her boss. "Too stubborn for her own good. My cousin Julio knows everybody around here who counts. Him and his boys practically live on the streets."

Behind Gloria, Annie was making a face and shaking her head.

Knowing Julio headed a local Hispanic gang, an amused Nick said, "I'll keep that in mind, Gloria, thanks."

"Humph." Gloria gave Annie a triumphant smile and said, "Some people know how to appreciate the offer of help. Well, I gotta get going." She turned her wicked gaze back at Nick. "Good luck, amigo. And you need me for anything, remember I'm in the book. Delgado. D-E-L-G-A-D-O."

Nick gave her a thumbs-up and she sashayed out the door, giving him a big wink before exiting into the night, crossing paths with a young woman who was entering the café wearing jeans, T-shirt, baseball cap and carrying a backpack.

Nick returned his attention to his friends and said, "Look, the truth is, I want out." Not that he would admit he was running scared. "I want nothing to do with Isabel Grayson, and I expect the two of you, as my best buddies, to talk me out of doing something stupid and against my better judgment."

Before either Helen or Annie could speak, the newcomer whomped her backpack on the table and said, "You want out before we even begin? You can't mean that, Nick. You gave me your word, and you're my last hope!"

Nick bit back a groan.

From beneath the baseball cap, Isabel Grayson herself was glaring at him, her eyes blazing blue fire.

"ISABEL, YOU'RE HERE."

Nick sounded startled and maybe sorry, no doubt because she'd overheard him trying to find a way to weasel out of helping her.

"*I'm* here," she said, looking around the table at his accomplices. "What about you?"

The blonde whom Isabel had spoken to when she'd left her card for Nick—Helen, wasn't it?—shot up out of her chair.

"Don't give me another thought," Helen said. "I'm gone." She grabbed the smaller woman's arm and pulled her to her feet. "We're both gone. C'mon, Annie, let's let them work this thing out."

Isabel waited until his friends had left before asking, "Is there anything to work out, Nick?" She tried not to let her heart bleed into her voice. "Or have you made up your mind?"

"Sit down, Isabel."

Nick appeared uncomfortable, even guilty. Good!

"I don't want to sit," she said. "I want to get out there and look for my sister. Nick, please."

She would get down on her knees and beg if she had to. No, not beg. Give him the blow job of his life. That might do it, since sex seemed to count with him. Right there, right now, she would shut her mind to the humiliation and do it if she thought it would work.

"You and me together," Nick said, "not the smartest move."

"There is no you and me. I am not romanticizing this. We're not anything but business partners. You made the rules. I agreed. I even proved that I would come through with my end of the deal, for God's sake!"

Though he looked as if he had something to say about that, Nick kept inordinately silent. She read his expression as pained.

Heartsick, wondering what the hell she was supposed to do now, Isabel backed off. "All right. I can't force you to come with me. Just promise me one thing." She'd told her father she could keep him quiet, but could she? "Forget I ever came to you and told you about Louise."

He narrowed his gaze on her. "And what are you going to do?"

"Find my sister."

"You already tried."

"I never tried living on the streets before. You convinced me that's what I had to do."

"Not alone!"

"That wasn't the plan. But now what choice do you leave me?"

"Go to the authorities or get a private investigator, the way you should have the moment you realized Louise wasn't bunking with a friend."

Isabel shook her head, grabbed her backpack and turned away from Nick. Because there was nothing more to say, she started to leave. She'd barely taken three steps before he'd caught up to her, his hand wrapped around her upper arm like a vise.

"You can't do this alone," he said.

"Probably not."

"You're crazy if you try."

"Probably so."

"You could get hurt."

She stared at him for a moment before asking, "What the hell do you care what happens to me?"

He didn't answer directly. "Your mind is set?"

"Like cement."

He cursed under his breath and, hand still surrounding her upper arm, headed for the door. "Then let's get out of here."

The change in Nick's attitude was so sudden that it made Isabel's head whirl and her eyes sting with unshed tears. She wanted to say something. To thank him. To make him promise he would see this through to success.

In the end she said nothing, merely caught back a

sob of relief and let him push her out the door and onto the dark streets that were to be her new home.

SENATOR WILLIAM GRAYSON looked around the room at the three men who worked most closely with him and tried to discern their degrees of loyalty in this matter.

He knew Jeff Enger still dreamed of running his own campaign. He would lose. No charisma. Enger knew that as well as he, the reason the man was still at the same job for more than a decade, the reason he would orchestrate the coming Senate race for him.

Enger's assistant, handsome young Danny Mc-Nulty, with his reddish-brown hair and twinkling green eyes, was an up-and-coming political personality. He was champing at the bit to be off and running. Another year and McNulty would be gone, probably running for a city office of his own. The charismatic Irishman might even make mayor someday.

And then there was Boyd, who had befriended his daughters and seemed content with his position dealing with the press. But Grayson knew better—though he didn't show his private face to the world, Boyd was the most ambitious of the bunch. And the most clever. He didn't mind remaining behind the scenes and knew exactly how to play people to get exactly what he wanted.

Yes, Grayson thought, he knew them all, knew their loyalty extended as far as keeping hushed what he didn't want the public to know. And this was, by far, the most potentially explosive situation he'd ever been in.

Rather, caught in.

Resting his elbows on his desk, Grayson sat forward and cleared his throat. "Gentlemen, we have a problem."

"I assume you mean Louise," Boyd said.

Grayson nodded. "And Isabel. She's brought a liability into the mix." He explained the problem, starting with the reason Louise ran and ending with Nick Novak's past with his daughter and the way that sorry affair had ended. "I wouldn't doubt that Novak is out for revenge of some sort. No doubt he'll get his licks in where he can, so the less he knows, the better. That means we need a quick fix, gentlemen, before he knows too much. We need to get right on this situation before it spirals out of our control."

"I'll see that it's taken care of," Enger promised.

As usual.

Grayson knew he could count on his chief of staff to come through for him. He could count on them all since they needed his approval and support.

"How do you want it handled?"

Grayson explained exactly what he had in mind.

"NAH, HAVEN'T SEEN HER," Kyle said, returning the photograph of Louise to Isabel, who tucked it in a zippered pocket of her backpack.

Kyle was one of the first runaways Nick had videotaped. Giving Isabel the once-over, the kid didn't bother hiding his suspicious expression. Neither did his companions, who stood back near the elevated rapid-transit structure and watched them warily, as if ready to run for their lives.

It was something they very well might have to do before the night was out, Nick knew. Kids on the street were vulnerable. Targets to all kinds of predators.

"She's my sister," Isabel said. "Please—she really needs me."

"I said, I haven't seen her!"

Nick put an arm around Isabel's shoulders and gave her a fast squeeze to keep her from pursuing what Kyle might know. As frightened and desperate as she was, she might scare off a potential lead.

He had to be careful, especially because her being so close was putting him off his game. From the moment he'd taken a good look at her in those soft, tight jeans, he'd had one thought on his mind. For a moment, their purpose faded and all he could think about was getting inside those jeans and burying himself in her...

Then, as if she knew what he was thinking, she pinched him surreptitiously and glared at him.

He blinked and came out of the sexual fog and back to reality. Back to the kid he'd come to care about.

"So, Kyle," he said, letting his genuine concern color his words, "have you spoken to your parents lately?"

"What for?" Though Kyle put on a tough facade, he couldn't hide the vulnerability that hid in his sixteen-year-old heart. "Same old, same old."

Nick nodded. "Keep your eyes and ears open for Louise, would you? You have my number." Nick slipped a twenty into the kid's hand. "And get some real food for all of you," he said, indicating the others. "No drugs."

"You know I don't do drugs anymore," Kyle said, giving Isabel a nervous glance.

Though Nick knew that Kyle was lying, probably for Isabel's sake—maybe he thought she would make him—he didn't contradict the kid.

"I'll get the word out," Kyle promised. "I hear anything, I'll let you know."

"Thanks, Kyle. And anytime you change your mind about that shelter, you let me know that, too."

"Nah, I'll take my chances on my own."

Knowing that all he could do was put out the offer, Nick clasped the kid's arm in farewell. Then he moved on down the pathway along the elevated structure toward the main drag, where runaways who'd done well on the streets would be spending their panhandled loot. Isabel slipped her backpack over her shoulders and kept right up with him.

"That didn't exactly go well."

"The night is young. Did you really think the first person we spoke to would lead us to her? Besides, even if Kyle did know something, he might not have spilled."

"Why not?" she asked, sounding appalled.

"You. They didn't trust you. I could see it in their expressions."

Isabel looked down at herself. "But I look just like them. No makeup, no fancy hair or outfit. I'm wearing Louise's clothes, for heaven's sake."

He followed her gaze and once again was struck

by how well those jeans fit her. Like a second skin. Skin he wanted to touch and taste.

Realizing she wasn't saying anything, he met her gaze, and for a moment, he thought she wanted that, too.

Mouth dry, he said, "But your clothes—they're clean and perfectly pressed. And that bulging backpack…" Nick shook his head. She really didn't understand that a desperate kid didn't take the time to pack before hitting the street. "Street-smart kids can spot a ringer a block away."

"A ringer?"

"Someone who thinks she can get something from them just by changing her appearance a little. Maybe it isn't enough."

"What do you want me to do? Roll around in some alley?"

He raised his eyebrows. "Hmm."

"I'll pass on that one."

"It's just that you look…too perfect."

"Perfect?"

"Here, maybe I can fix that." Nick reached over and swiped his hand along the soot-covered metal of the transit structure. Then after rubbing both hands together, he put one on the shoulder of her T-shirt. Her warmth bit him but he didn't flinch.

"Hey!" She immediately tried brushing the blotch away, but merely managed to smudge it.

"Even better," Nick told her. He tried to ignore the heat that had instantly flowed through his veins at their contact and centered itself in his groin. "More natural. Now you don't look quite so perfect."

"One daub of dirt is going to make all the difference in the world, right?"

"Not exactly. It takes work to stay clean when you're on the streets."

Ever so lightly, he brushed her cheek with his thumb and was jolted by the sensation that whipped through him. It took all his willpower not to go further, not to trail his fingers down her neck and to her breasts. They strained against the T-shirt, and he couldn't miss the way her nipples hardened at his touch.

Wiping her hand across her cheek only managed to lighten, not erase the swipe of grime he'd left there. Even though it was nearly dark, he could see her glare as she asked, "You're enjoying this, aren't you?"

"This?" he echoed. No, *enjoy* was the wrong word, because he was becoming more and more conflicted about what he was doing. Though he might want her—against his will!—he didn't want to force her into anything. "You mean trying to find a kid in trouble?"

"I mean torturing me while you're at it."

"I wouldn't call that torture," he said, now amused. "So, if you want—"

"No. Thanks. I'll pass." She walked with him along the tracks silently for a moment, then said, "That kid, Kyle. What's his story?"

"Bad home life." Kyle had only asked him not to contact his parents or the authorities in return for his cooperation, which was a typical concern of a kid on the street, as Nick knew so well. "His mother is into recreational drugs. She was high and driving with his little brother in the car when she had an accident. The kid's dead, the mother wasn't even hurt. No one figured out she was on drugs and the father isn't doing anything to get her into rehab.''

''How tragic for them all!'' Isabel said, sounding appalled. ''But no one can force a person to get help. Well, maybe a court order.''

''The father could try talking her into going there,'' Nick said grimly. ''Kyle says he won't go back unless things change at home.''

''And now Kyle is on the street and does drugs himself.''

''Though I don't think as often as he used to,'' Nick said, hoping he was right. ''He admitted he learned to do them with his mom when he walked in on her and she shared her stash to keep him quiet.''

''Jesus!''

''Shocked?'' Considering the intensity of her response, Isabel really must be more sheltered than he'd realized. ''Why do you think kids run? Because they have great home lives?''

''I guess I never actually thought that closely about it before.''

''Well, start thinking,'' he muttered, then added, ''since you're one person who might actually be able to do something to turn things around for these kids.''

''Through my father, you mean.''

''What about through *you?*''

''I have no power. And my father does some good, you know,'' Isabel said, sounding defensive. ''You may have reason for disliking him, but he's done a lot for this city and state. And this country, too. He's worked for school reform and day care and legal representation for the elderly.''

"Good. Then he should certainly be interested in the growing runaway issue.''

Isabel didn't say anything. Helping homeless teens was obviously something that didn't interest her father or her, Nick decided. These kids had no voting power, especially not the young ones. He didn't push. He'd just wait and let her see how desperate a person could get on the street. And then maybe she would see her way to taking action.

"Where are we going now?'' she asked.

"I know a couple of places on Milwaukee Avenue where teens hang out.''

"You mean runaways.''

"Some. They don't have official gathering spots or wear signs identifying themselves. They try to fit in as long as they can.''

"And then what happens? What changes?''

"They do,'' Nick said, as dark memories rushed over him.

4

A FRISSON OF FEAR SLID DOWN Isabel's spine at Nick's dire tone. She wasn't afraid for herself, but for Louise, and all those kids trying to take care of themselves and being forced to the dark side to do so.

Somehow, Nick thought she could help, and something in her responded to that belief. Her father rarely gave her credit, and only as it applied to working for him.

But what could she do to make a difference?

Isabel thought about it as she followed Nick onto Milwaukee Avenue, but drew a blank.

They headed for the bright lights of the six corners where Nick did business and lived. Now the area was crowded with people coming in and out of restaurants or shops. Tourists mingled with the unwashed—and the highly made-up, she thought, amused as a mime tried to get a handout from a designer-dressed middle-aged woman who looked aghast.

They continued on southeast. A little more than a block down they came to a business called Eye-Candy, a combination tattoo-and-piercing parlor and eyeglasses and jewelry boutique. The place also boasted a juice bar.

Nick placed an arm around her back and turned her into the doorway. Isabel felt her knees weaken as she took the lead into the busy shop with him right behind her, so close that she could feel his body heat along the length of her back and his breath ruffling her hair. Gasping, she took a fast step forward that loosened his hold on her. He let go, but still she felt the lingering impact of his fingers on her flesh.

"Juice bar," he said, moving toward the back corner where a blender whirred noisily.

Following at her own pace as he sidled up to the bar, Isabel took a quick look around her and noted how young the customers seemed to be. And the employees. She and Nick were the oldest people there.

She kept looking, wondering if these were regular kids with homes—like the girl getting the butterfly tattooed on her shoulder or the guy having his tongue pierced. Grimacing at the last, she glanced away to the knot of girls giggling together as they tried on funky eyewear.

They were so damn young! she thought, backing up toward the juice bar. Younger than Louise even. Surely *they* weren't on their own? Suddenly she slammed into another body and when she turned to apologize, Nick handed her a shot glass.

"To good health," he toasted.

"What is it?"

"Just drink up. It's good for you. You'll need the energy."

Isabel eyed the murky liquid of indeterminate color suspiciously. "Do I have to?"

Nick gave her a look and downed his own concoction. Making a face but determined that he wouldn't outdo her, Isabel followed suit.

"Yuk. This stuff is safe, right?"

Nick arched his brows. "You'll have to let me know if you feel any side effects." Then he added, "It's wheat grass. I promise it'll only do you good."

Isabel had never been into health-food products and was somewhat surprised that Nick was. Then, why should she be? From the looks of his torso and arms—not to mention the well-developed six-pack—he obviously believed his body was his temple. She couldn't help but wonder what the lower regions looked like, now that Nick was a fully mature man.

That thought placed Isabel smack in a discomfort zone she couldn't seem to climb out of for more than a few minutes at a time. When Nick took her glass and his hand brushed hers, she blamed the wheat grass for setting her insides on fire. He put her glass down on the counter next to his and she waited for her insides to steady.

"What now?" she asked breathlessly.

"We shop and chat." He pulled her closer to the girl whose tattoo was almost finished.

The butterfly was beautiful and lifelike, Isabel thought.

"A tattoo would look good on you," Nick murmured in her hair. "How about a little heart on your... well, in a place where not everyone could see it?"

It had to be the wheat grass making her pulse kick up at his suggestion, Isabel thought, because, for a moment, she considered it. "What would be the point of that?"

"It would be a little secret just for you...and someone close to you...."

She glanced back at him so close she could feel his body heat, and raised her eyebrows. "And who might that be?"

When he blanched, she grinned.

Suddenly Isabel realized the significance of their presence at this place, and her rising tension shifted in a new direction. "You think Louise got herself tattooed and pierced here?"

"Would the senator disown her if she did something to herself that didn't meet with his approval?"

Even though her father could be blunt about his dislikes and didn't hesitate to use any leverage at his disposal to get what he wanted, that applied to big issues, not small ones like tattoos.

"Why would you think that?" she asked.

"*Why* is definitely the question. As in...why did Louise run?"

Uh-oh, she'd known this was coming. "I told you—"

"Nothing of substance."

Nor would she, at least not yet.

How would Nick react if she told him everything about Louise's running away? And how could she when she didn't trust him?

Besides, she truly hadn't decided what to do with the information that could jeopardize her father's stellar political career, could end the good things he did for people. The trade-off was unthinkable, the position he'd placed her in, untenable.

And Nick *would* have to be her solution...he and his bargain.

Though part of her dreaded going through with the agreement, Isabel acknowledged the underlying excitement she felt at being with him again. At the idea of their sating themselves with each other night after night. No sex had ever come close to what she'd had with him.

Maybe it was because they'd been so damn young and careful with each other. Maybe because they'd learned to explore each other's bodies, to satisfy each other in numerous ways before they'd actually slept together. Maybe because they'd been in love.

Whatever the reason, something akin to the sense of adventure and danger she'd felt as a teenager when she'd defied her father to see the oh-so-inappropriate Nick Novak had taken hold of her once more.

Therein lay her problem with him: she couldn't forget how bitterly their short-lived Romeo-and-Juliet romance had ended.

And, she was certain, even more important, he wouldn't have, either, because it had been her fault.

"So are you going to spill or what?"

Nick's breath spilled over the shell of her ear as he made the demand, his shoulder pressing into the back of hers. Her backpack prevented full body contact. Thankfully. Shivering, Isabel turned her head to meet his gaze. They were so close she should have been able to see inside him, but he wouldn't let her in, wouldn't let her see the real man.

What had Nick grown into? Isabel wondered, hoping he was a man who put honor before vengeance, but fearing he wasn't.

"Later," she said, turning her attention to the tattoo artist, who was putting the finishing touches on the butterfly. The woman was as interesting to look at as her work. Her short hair was spiked and the same glossy red and black as her midriff-length blouse. Isabel noted her navel ring with what looked like a black diamond.

"That's it, sweetheart, enjoy." The tattoo artist sent the client on her way and turned to them. "Nick!" Her dark eyes widened behind tiny horn-rimmed glasses. "You've finally succumbed to my talent."

"No, Roberta, we're looking for someone who might have come by for some work in the last week," Nick said smoothly. "A seventeen-year-old girl."

Roberta rolled her eyes. "Never seen one of those in *he-e-ere.*"

"Her name is Louise and she's a pretty blonde like her sister here. Take a look at the picture," Nick said, indicating Isabel should whip it out of her backpack.

A moment later, the tattooist studied the photo, then shook her head. "Nope. Never seen her, Nick, darling. Someone as delicious as this one I would remember."

But Roberta was looking straight at Isabel, who shifted uncomfortably.

Nick said, "You keep an eye out for Louise and you'll have my undying gratitude."

Roberta pouted. "Is that all I get?" She looked

from one to the other, her expression sly. "And what do I get if I find her for you?"

"I'd say name it, but you might take advantage."

Nick said it with such good humor that Roberta smacked him lightly in the chest, then let her inch-long nails trail over the musculature.

"You know I'm your adoring slave."

A new customer cut off any further banter.

As they moved on to the ear-piercing area, Isabel whispered, "She swings both ways, huh?"

"No," Nick murmured into her ear. "*He* does. Roberta used to be Robert."

Isabel laughed. "TMI—too much information."

A little too unusual for her. She had to admit she was something of a conservative in a democratic world. Even her father chastised her at times for not being more open.

Once she *had* been open and trusting, Isabel remembered. And then she had met Nick Novak. And the way that relationship had ended had affected her so deeply that she herself had changed forever.

THEY LEFT EYE-CANDY AFTER getting a lead from a girl Nick had interviewed weeks ago. She'd suggested he check out Wicker Park. There was a whole neighborhood in the city that went by that name, but she meant the actual park. She'd heard about a new girl who'd been hanging out there for the past couple of nights. And if he didn't have any luck at that park, she'd mentioned another nearby.

As they walked down a side street, Nick thought about how he would give his eyeteeth to know what

Isabel was hiding from him. He could insist on the truth, the whole truth and nothing but the truth. He could tell her that he wouldn't go another step unless she revealed everything that had happened to make Louise flee. No doubt Isabel was protecting her father from some form of political suicide...but what was it, exactly? Louise hadn't run merely because she was out of line and her father had put some restrictions on her. Of that he was certain.

He feared that if he gave Isabel an ultimatum, though, she would walk away from him forever. Nick started when he realized how much that thought bothered him.

But that was what he wanted, wasn't it? He'd even tried to enlist Helen's and Annie's help to get rid of her. So why did he hesitate now? He could push Isabel until she couldn't be pushed any more, and then she would make the decision to walk away and he would be free of her forever.

Or would he ever be free?

It had taken him a hell of a long time—years, in fact—but he'd finally thought he was free. Clearly he wasn't finished with her, though, or he wouldn't be walking around with a hard-on like some green kid waiting to dip his wick for the first time.

His first time had been with Isabel. He'd been eighteen and maybe the last guy in school to get it on with a chick. They'd spent weeks working up to it. Furtive meetings in hidden corners during which she would let him touch her and she would touch him in return. They'd burned for each other and had taken every opportunity to explore each other.

Isabel had been the first girl to go down on him.

The first girl he'd tasted.

The first and only girl to ever give him her virginity.

Maybe that was his problem, first times having some special hold on a person. Maybe once he had Isabel again, he would get it through his head that she was nothing special.

And that she was nothing to him, nor he to her, exactly as she'd told him that last time he'd seen her, Nick remembered. Exactly as she'd told him in front of her *real* friends when he'd gone to find her because he'd been in a serious crisis and had needed someone who cared about him to listen.

"These streets are kind of spooky," Isabel said, moving a little closer to him.

Nick caught his breath. He *wasn't* done with her, no matter how much he wanted to be. But he would be, he promised himself. He would get her out of his system.

"Don't worry. You're safe with me." At least in the literal sense.

The neighborhood was neat, nearly litter-free, mostly old houses built before the streets had been raised at the turn of the century. What had once been high first floors were now at sidewalk level, and some of the gardens were still "sunken." Landfill had brought others to sidewalk level. Old the homes might be, but they were well taken care of or rehabbed, and there were a few new buildings in between. But this block wasn't particularly well lit—lots of big old trees hid the streetlights. Ahead, a couple of guys, maybe in their early twenties, leaned against an iron fence and smoked and argued in low, intense tones.

Just guys, Nick decided, though they probably seemed more threatening to a woman used to a better neighborhood. If she was nervous here, just wait, did she have another think coming or what! Glancing at her, he realized she was more uptight than normal.

"Here," he said.

Some rusty sense of chivalry make him slip an arm around her waist and draw her closer to make her feel more secure.

Torture. He must be into torture. His sudden arousal throbbed with every step they took and urged him to abandon the search and find a place to take her and get it over with. He imagined entering her, making her moan with pleasure....

Hanging on to the control that supposedly meant he still held on to a thread of decency, he told her, "These streets are as safe as any in the city."

"If you say so."

Isabel was wired with tension that came at him in waves. When he gave her a reassuring squeeze, she relaxed a bit, and when they passed the smoking duo without incident, she relaxed some more, her fleshy curves pressing into his more intimately.

Yep, torture...

Nick eyed a garden arbor, wondering if he could guide her into there for a private moment, but he kept himself in check. *Later,* he promised himself. Later, he would have her any way he wanted her and then whatever spell she'd had him under for so long would be broken.

They rounded a corner and came in sight of the park. A fountain burbled near the small field house, and a half-dozen teenagers sprawled around a picnic table on its other side. Isabel's steps quickened and Nick lengthened his stride to keep up with her. He was still too far away to see anyone clearly, but chances were that finding Louise wasn't going to be this easy.

Equally certain that Isabel had her hopes high at the moment, he figured he'd better be ready for her crash of disappointment if nothing came of the encounter.

ISABEL SLOWED HER STEPS as they drew closer to the teenagers and she could see that Louise was not among them. Fighting disappointment, she kept her calm and stopped a short distance from the group.

"Excuse me, I'm looking for my sister," she said as he drew closer to her. "Her name is Louise. Her friends call her Lulu."

Nick started, then glanced at her sharply at this information but when she gave him a look, he let it go and turned his attention to the teenagers.

"Maybe your sister isn't looking for *you*," said a dark-skinned girl whose intricately braided hair hung over her shoulders.

They all laughed.

"Not funny," Nick said. He recognized a couple of the kids. One was a runaway he'd videotaped. "Some of you know me, right? I can vouch for this woman. Her sister doesn't need to be on the street. They can work it out."

Isabel felt the shift in attitude and quickly took up where he left off. "Louise visited a friend in this neighborhood a few days ago. I was hoping she might still be hanging out around here."

After retrieving the photo, she held it out, but no one would take it from her. One couple looked away, then actually locked lips and began making out as if she didn't exist.

"I just want her to be safe," Isabel told them. "I want her to come home."

"We can't all have what we want, now, can we?"

That from a too thin girl whose pale hair shone a strange shade of silver under the park's mercury-vapor lights. Her face was caked with makeup that didn't quite hide bruising. Was she running from the person who'd hit her, Isabel wondered, or had that happened out here on the streets? She imagined this, rather than Louise, might be the "new" girl.

Disappointed, she held out Louise's photo to the girl. "I love my sister and I only want the best for her. Just look at this, please."

The girl took it and stared for a moment. "She kind of looks familiar, but she hasn't been hanging with us."

"But you think you've seen her? Where?"

The girl shrugged. "I—I can't be sure…maybe at Club Undercover. Mondays and Thursdays they have an early liquor-free gathering for underage kids."

"Do you know the place?" Isabel asked Nick.

"Oh, yeah."

Isabel's hope renewed. "If you see Louise, would you tell her I'm looking for her?"

"You got some kind of reward?" one of the boys asked.

"Depends on how accurate the tip," Nick said. "If any of you helps us find her, how does a C-note sound? Nick's Knack—that's my business up the block at the six corners."

"I remember," the black girl said. "Second floor over Annie's Attic. You ever do anything with that video?"

"I'm making editing notes," he told her. "And still shooting. I promise, when I'm all done I'll spread the word and have a special showing for everyone who contributed."

How had she lost control? Isabel wondered.

"Will there be food?" the thin girl asked, making Isabel swallow hard at the thought that she was probably hungry.

Nick said, "As much as you can eat."

Isabel pulled a twenty out of her pocket the way Nick had earlier.

"It's not much, but it'll get you some fast food."

She held out the bill to the too thin girl, who hesitated only a moment before snatching it out of her hand. She seemed ashamed, Isabel thought. She was only a kid, maybe fifteen, maybe younger. What were her resources if she couldn't go home?

"Thanks," the girl muttered, her eyes cast downward.

"Hey, what about me?" one of the guys said.

"I'll share with anyone who's hungry," the girl offered.

Hot tears seared the backs of Isabel's eyelids. Hunger was nothing to joke about.

Was her sister hungry? Had she run out of money yet? Louise did have a credit card, Isabel told herself. Surely she would have the sense to use it to buy food, if not to pay for a hotel room.

And surely she herself could figure out something she could do to help halt the problem, Isabel thought. She might not know anything about videos, but she was a writer, after all, considering all the press releases she created for her father.

As they reached the western edge of the park, Isabel said, "You have quite a rapport with these kids."

"No big deal."

"Yes, it is. It's as if…they know you."

"Some of them do," he reminded her. "I've been on the street myself."

"Videotaping them."

Nick hesitated only a moment before saying, "Right. Videotaping them."

They were back on Damen, heading for the six corners again.

"What now?" Isabel asked.

"Club Undercover."

"But it's not Monday or Thursday. No teenagers."

"But I know the owner," Nick explained. "I do some video work for the club."

"Oh. Then he's a good resource."

"You don't sound too enthusiastic."

"It's late." She was distracted, worrying about the kids and sensing danger everywhere. First the guys smoking, then the kids, then some guy who'd seemed to be a half block back for a while now—of course, he was likely just another guy from the neighborhood. "I'm a little tired, is all."

"Ready to turn in for the night?"

The way he said it in that low tone made her flesh prickle and her mouth go dry. It set off alarms in her body...and in her head.

"Not yet," she said breathlessly, imagining the demands he might make of her. As the hour drew near, thoughts of the night ahead grew more potent. "Not until we run out of leads."

Certain that Nick was anxious for his damn trade-off, Isabel thought he should just wait for it.

She wondered how long she could stall him. Long enough that Nick would be so tired he would rather sleep than have sex? Probably not. He was probably pumped for it—looking forward to humiliating her, to settling their score.

And part of her thought she deserved it. She hadn't had to be so cruel to him, she admitted to herself. But the practical part of her wondered how else she could have done what she'd had to do.

So she would let him have his revenge, if that would even out things in his mind.

And he would lead her to her sister.

A business deal, that's how she would have to think of what she'd agreed to. The kind of deal she often found herself involved in for political expediency. Not that anyone else had ever demanded anything so personal from her.

But everything was a trade-off in politics and in life—at least in *her* life—it seemed. No matter how pure your motives were when you started out, you couldn't get anything done unless you were willing to compromise. She heard her father's voice in her head—he'd said those words or ones like them too many times for her to forget.

So that's how she would think of her night with Nick.

A compromise. Sensible. Businesslike.

But Isabel had to admit the thought of getting naked with the only man who'd ever held the key to her heart wasn't feeling much like business. She got turned on by his touch. His voice. The way he looked at her. All of them were too devastatingly familiar. The night held disaster, she feared. She might stall him as long as she could, but, deep inside, a longing she'd buried for years was resurfacing. A longing that would get her nothing but more heartbreak.

They were moving along Milwaukee again before he interrupted her confused thoughts. "Lulu...why didn't you tell me Louise went by a nickname?"

Realizing he sounded put out, she said, "I simply didn't think of it."

"How many more details have skipped your mind?" Nick asked. "The more information I have about the *whole* situation, the better."

Right. He wanted her to spill. About her father.

Well, she would...in her own time.... When she was ready...maybe....

But only if she was certain Nick could be trusted to keep secret information that could ruin the man who'd once been the ruin of *them*.

THEY WERE TAKING HIM in circles and his nerves were definitely on edge. So far they hadn't made him, but unless something happened soon, it was only a matter of time.

Only a matter of time until they led him to the brat, he reminded himself, popping a pill that would take off the edge.

That one would be the ruin of everything unless he stopped her. Surely he could talk to her, make her see reason. No need for her to make such a big fuss about things that really didn't affect her directly. He would convince her that what she knew could stay between those involved.

Kids liked keeping secrets. She was just a little freaked out, was all.

With the right coaxing, she would come around.

She had better…

5

NICK WASN'T CERTAIN EXACTLY when he'd realized they were being followed. The guy hadn't been overt, hadn't gotten too close. He'd let others coming and going get between them. But for blocks now, he'd been there. He'd obviously seen a target in them.

More the fool was he.

No one was more street-smart than he himself was, Nick thought. Not that the guy would be aware of that. So, if he was out for easy pickings—Isabel's backpack or his own wallet—the guy was in for a surprise.

Or might there be another reason for their being followed? he wondered. Maybe he needed to find out for sure.

"How much farther?" Isabel asked, her exhaustion, which was probably more mental than physical, clear in her plea.

"The club is just ahead at the end of the block."

Nick glanced back casually, his gaze only touching the guy following them before he faced forward. Not too big or scary looking. Not too badly dressed, either—dark pants and shirt and a dark, billed cap pulled low to conceal his face.

Could be anyone.

Certain that he could take the guy, Nick looked for an opportunity to confront him on his own terms. Not long after, he saw it directly ahead.

Taking Isabel's arm, he softly said, "Just do what I say and don't fight me."

"What are you up to?"

"This."

He ducked into an alley, taking her with him and pulling her back out of harm's way. He put a finger to his lips and indicated she should stay put as he prepared to spring in front of the guy who was following them and find out what the hell he wanted.

"Nick," she complained in a whisper.

He put his finger to his mouth again. Then he prepared himself mentally. He was strong and fast, but, more important, he'd had enough street altercations to value the element of surprise.

The mouth of the alley became his entire focus. His body was on high alert—when he heard a noise from somewhere behind. The second he let his focus waver was a second too long. The guy who'd been following them crossed their path, and before Nick could even get a good look at him, he was knocked into by a big, soft body, one that reeked of alcohol and other strange odors.

"Wha' the hell you think you're doin'?" the drunk asked as he grabbed the front of Nick's T-shirt and tried shoving him into the brick wall.

"Damn!"

Nick knocked the drunk out of the way, grabbed Isabel's hand and shot out onto the sidewalk. It was too late. A group of noisy twenty-somethings emptied out of a nearby restaurant, blocking his view. He fought through them, but it was a losing battle. Somewhere on the other side, the guy who'd been following him and Isabel had been swallowed by some doorway or vehicle.

Turning to Isabel, who'd been muttering in annoyance at his manhandling, he said, "Vanished."

"Who?"

"The guy who was following us."

"Then I—I wasn't imagining things."

"You knew and you didn't say anything?"

"What about you?" she asked, sounding offended. "Why didn't you tell me?"

"I wasn't sure."

"Or was it you don't trust me?"

Isabel shoved him in the chest and tried to move past him, but Nick caught her and twirled her around to face him. He cradled her lightly in his arms. She was upset. And she had every right to be.

"Where do you think you're going?"

"To find my sister."

"I thought you couldn't do it without me. I thought you needed me."

He could see she was barely holding on to it. Even under the streetlights, he could see her eyes looked glazed, as if she were ready to cry. Damn, he couldn't stand to see a woman cry! He wanted to pull her closer and crush her to him, but that might make her even angrier.

Instead, he tried to ease her mind. "Look, it's not a matter of trust," he said softly. "I'm just not used to consulting a partner, okay?"

Isabel swallowed hard and blinked. "Okay."

Her eyes were damp, as were her parted lips. Full, tempting lips. It took every ounce of willpower he possessed not to kiss them and shatter the fragile truce.

"Let's get over to Club Undercover and see what Gideon has to say."

"Gideon?"

"The owner."

"And personal friend?"

"Sometimes employer. I'm not sure Gideon has friends."

"How sad."

"How about you, Isabel?" he asked as they continued along the street. He swept his gaze over every inch of the vicinity but didn't see the guy who'd been following them. "Do you have any friends? I mean *real friends,* not just political allies or socially correct acquaintances."

"My college roommate—at least between men. Nora tends to concentrate primarily on whomever she's dating. There used to be four of us who hung out together and vacationed together, but Cynthia got married last year, Jennie the year before. That changed things, but I guess that's normal when you have someone special in your life."

Which meant she didn't, at least not at the moment. Now, why did that make him feel so great? he mused, turning her into the doorway of the club.

Isabel had already pulled herself together, so there was no hint of the uncertain woman he'd seen a moment ago. Spooky how she could transform herself on a dime, a talent she'd had even as a teenager, he remembered.

If he didn't know her better, she might even be able to fool him.

ISABEL LET NICK GUIDE HER down to the dark, cavernous, smoky space, pulsating with loud music.

"Hey, Nicky, can I get you a table?" the attractive purple-haired hostess asked.

"Sweet of you, Mags, but I'm here to see the boss if he's available."

"I'll find out." Mags picked up her station phone. "'Nicky'?"

"Mags is very friendly," Nick explained.

"I'll just bet she is."

How friendly? Isabel wondered. Friendly enough to have been one of Nick's options for the night if he wasn't stuck with her?

Not that she gave a damn.

Before she had the opportunity to ask, Mags said, "He'll see you. Go on in."

"Thanks."

As Nick swept her past the entryway of the club, Isabel barely got a glimpse of its huge video screen, dance floor and raised seating in the back. The music followed them but tapered off in intensity as they headed down a hall. Nick stopped at one of the doors and knocked.

As Nick entered the modern office, decorated with jewel-tone blue walls and black-and-chrome furniture, the man behind the desk said, "Come on in."

Gideon was as dark as Nick was fair. His blue-black hair was long, smoothed back from his classi- cally handsome face and curled slightly at the nape of his neck. Eyes the deepest blue she'd ever seen seemed to strip her down and inspect her carefully.

"Nick, good to see you," the club owner said, though he was still staring directly at her as if he were trying to see through her disguise. "And this lovely lady might be…?"

"Isabel Grayson."

Isabel started at the revelation of her last name and surreptitiously poked Nick in the ribs. "Can I speak to you a moment?" she whispered. "Alone!"

"One minute," Nick said to Gideon as he stepped back into the hall with her.

"You told him who I was!" Isabel accused him angrily.

"You have to tell him everything you know if you want his help," Nick said reasonably. "Yes or no?"

She glanced back inside. "Not if the price is too high. What were you thinking?" she admonished.

"That Gideon is the soul of discretion and what you tell him stays with him," Nick promised her. "He has no use for the media other than to publicize his club—believe me."

Isabel wanted to believe him. Wanted to believe this Gideon might be able to help. "I hope you're right."

"Trust me."

What else could she do now that the cat was out of the bag? She nodded.

"Sorry," Nick told Gideon as he strolled back in- side, Isabel following reluctantly.

"Sit," Gideon said. "Can I get you a drink?"

"Not for me," she said.

"Me, neither."

"Then what *can* I get you?"

"Information," Nick said

"About?"

"A girl who might be hanging around with the Monday and Thursday crowd."

"How old?"

"Seventeen."

"What does she look like?"

"Me." Realizing Gideon might not know who she was, after all, a relieved Isabel offered the photo. "My sister, Louise."

Gideon nodded. "I did see her in here the other night."

"How can you be sure?"

"I am blessed with a photographic memory. I never forget a face."

"You spend that much time in the club and you would know every face you saw?"

"I make the rounds often enough," Gideon said, handing back the likeness of Louise. "I keep my finger on the pulse of the place, so to speak."

"Can you find her? Or lead us to someone who can?"

"I'm not a miracle worker. If she's on the street—"

Disappointed, Isabel started to rise, saying, "Well, thanks, anyway."

"Hold on, Miss Grayson." Gideon sat back in his

chair, elbows on the arms, fingers steepled together. "I didn't say I couldn't help you."

Afraid to hope, she asked, "How?"

"Do you have copies of that photo?"

"No, I suppose I should have made some."

"Then, to start," he said, sitting forward, "I can make copies, pass them around to my staff and have them keep an eye out for your sister."

"But the next teen night isn't until tomorrow," Isabel stated bluntly.

"Perhaps you won't find her before then."

No doubt he was right, Isabel thought, wondering how many days she would be spending in Nick's company.

And how many nights?

Flushing at the thought of how she would keep Nick satisfied, Isabel nodded. "All right."

"And you should take extra copies to hand out on the street, as well. I assume you have a cell phone."

"Of course. I need to be able take calls that might be important. I'm hoping my sister will still call me."

"So what aren't you telling me?" Gideon asked.

Isabel gave Nick a sharp look. Surely he wasn't going to tell this man about their bargain.

"Louise is a runaway," he said. "Chances are, she's on the street, so that's where we need to be."

Gideon nodded. "Makes sense. But it surprises me, too."

"What does?" Isabel asked.

"That someone of your background would be willing to hit the streets."

He *did* know who she was, Isabel realized. Only

he hadn't mentioned it. Hadn't brought up her father's name once. In light of that, she had hopes that Gideon would indeed remain as discreet as Nick had indicated.

"Let's get started, then," Gideon said. "I'll need that photograph of Louise. And your cell phone number, as well."

She gave him both.

Surprisingly, Gideon didn't call a staff member to make the copies. He excused himself and said he would be back with what they needed in a few minutes.

A few *awkward* minutes.

Expecting Nick to renew the argument, Isabel waited, tense and expectant. But the argument didn't come. Nick didn't say a word. And when she looked at him, he seemed to be deep inside himself, in a place she couldn't touch.

Another thing she remembered about him.

In high school, he'd gone off into his own world, too, and there had been times she hadn't been able to reach him. He'd never explained, simply had told her it was a place she wouldn't want to visit.

Was he there now? she wondered. That same dark place?

Reaching out to him, she touched his arm. "Are you all right?"

He started and surprise crossed his features. "All right? Yeah, sure. Why wouldn't I be?"

He was lying. She could see it deep within his eyes before caution overtook him and he hid whatever he'd been feeling.

Before she could figure out how to approach him, Gideon was back with color copies of the photo. He gave her a handful, which she stuffed into her backpack after noticing that he'd added a note that anyone who saw the girl should call her cell phone number.

Not that Isabel was convinced she should use them—not yet. Advertising a missing kid and including a phone number that could be traced to its owner would nullify the precautions she'd taken. But she didn't say that, merely thanked Gideon for his help and asked that he only alert the members of his staff whom he knew would be discreet.

Back on the street, she wasn't sure what to expect, but if Nick were really angry with her, he wasn't showing it.

"What next?" he asked.

"That other park?"

"It's a walk."

"That's why I wore walking shoes. Unless you wanted to take a taxi…" Her words died under his stare.

"You really don't get it, do you?"

"What? Living on the streets? How would anyone know we took transportation to our next destination? We could get off a block before the park—"

"*We* would know." He started walking away from the club. "And you wouldn't get it any more than you do now."

"Wouldn't get what?" she asked, trying to keep up with him.

"The exhaustion…frustration…desperation." His

stride lengthened with each word. "The fear that no matter what you do, this is your life now."

For a moment, she imagined herself being in those shoes and those emotions flooded her.

"Okay, I'll walk. I *am* walking."

And she would continue to walk until she dropped if it helped her find Louise.

Then what?

Problem solving was her domain, it seemed, at least in the personal arena. But she found dealing with this latest crisis of her father's distasteful. All she wanted to do was find her sister and take her someplace where they didn't have to watch their every word, their every move. Where she didn't have to make nice to the press and misdirect them so that they didn't look for what her father didn't want them to know.

What she wanted for *herself,* at least, was a different world.

And yet not exactly.

Having the best part of her father in her, she wanted to do positive things for her community and for the people in it. That's why she'd stuck to her father's office for so long. Senator William Grayson had a fine record of public service, one of which she was proud. One she would like to emulate, if in a more forthright way.

Suddenly she realized that this was it, her opportunity. Nick was doing it—trying to make people aware of what it was like for kids on the street—so why couldn't she?

His forte was using a video camera, hers was using a pen. Well, a computer.

Having worked for her father for years, she had so many media contacts. Surely someone would be interested in a piece on runaways, especially if it was written from this side of the street.

Her excitement turned to guilt, though, when she thought about Louise. She certainly didn't mean to use her sister's plight for her own gain.

Right now, finding Louise should be her only goal.

As for her sister's future, Isabel didn't know what would be best. Their mother was busy with her political duties and charities and personal interests. Not that she wasn't interested in her children. She had simply never been a strong personality in her own right. Mother had never been able to handle Louise even when she tried her hardest. When Isabel had tried to broach the subject of her plan to find her sister, Mother had simply closed up and had taken to her room.

Maybe her sister going away to college in the fall would be the best thing, would get her away from their parents and give her time and space to find out who she was. And, until then, Isabel was willing to make alternative living arrangements if that's what it took to bring her home.

"Penny for your thoughts," Nick broke in.

"A penny doesn't buy much anymore."

"You sound tired. It's not all that much farther."

He sounded sympathetic and slid an arm around her back as if trying to support her. Appreciative, Isabel leaned in to his warmth and, for a moment, imagined they were just an ordinary couple walking down the street. When tears sprang to her eyes, she realized how very tired she was. She dashed them away with a shaky hand.

"If we don't get anything solid to follow, we can stop," he said, giving her side a squeeze.

"And sleep in the park?" she asked lightly, dreading the answer.

When he said, "Not tonight," she silently gave thanks for the reprieve.

"Where, then?" she asked, imagining he would give in and say they could sleep at his studio.

So when he casually stated, "An abandoned building that's about to be rehabbed," a knot formed in her stomach.

Visions of rats and other unwanted creatures dancing in her head, she asked, "Won't it be boarded up?"

"That won't be a problem."

Getting into a boarded-up building was not a problem?

Nick made it sound as if he'd done this kind of thing before, which was ridiculous, of course. But maybe he knew about the building from some runaway he'd taped, which would mean others might take shelter there.

Maybe even Louise.

She could only hope.

"Listen, Isabel, about that guy who was following us," Nick said, shaking her out of her thoughts. "You didn't get a look at him, did you?"

Immediately paranoid, she glanced over her shoulder and was relieved to see that the street behind them was empty. "No, not really. He was kind of nonde-script, and that hat hid his face. What about him?"

"It's possible he wasn't going to mug us."

"What, then?"

"Why did Louise run?"

"I told you—"

"I know what you told me. Nothing concrete."

She glanced at him, pretty sure she knew where he was going with this. "You think the guy following us has something to do with Louise."

"Since you won't be up-front about it, you would be a better judge of that than I."

"A reporter?"

Isabel thought that some reporter smelling a story and following her was a little far-fetched. A thief was far more plausible.

Either prospect bothered her all the way to their next destination.

This park was a big disappointment compared to the last. Really, it was only a play lot with swings, monkey bars and a sandbox. The only person there was an old guy stretched out on a bench, a black plastic bag of possessions under his head and another under his feet. They questioned him briefly, but if he'd seen anyone who looked like Louise, he wasn't telling.

Admitting they would do well to reconnoiter and set off again in daylight, Nick headed them toward the abandoned building, which he claimed was only a few blocks away. Isabel tried to clear her mind of what it and the night held for her.

6

WHEN THEY ARRIVED at the commercial building with
a Cornerstone Realty sign out front, it appeared more
amenable than Isabel had feared. Though her imagination had populated the place with rats and roaches,
it actually seemed fairly clean. Well, clean for an
abandoned commercial building in an edgy part of
town.

While she'd stood guard holding her backpack and
the sack of fast food Nick had bought on the way
here, he'd gone around back, where he'd jimmied
open a window, then had come around to let her in
through the front door.

They now stood in a main room, probably a former
reception area, barely lit by streetlights coming
through the grease-streaked windows. There was no
furniture to speak of, merely a counter behind which
she assumed there had once been desks.

She whipped out the Maglite she'd taken from her
backpack and turned it on, illuminating the floor. A
little crumbled plaster. Dust. Nothing horrendous.

The smell of the tacos Nick had bought on their
way over got to her and her empty stomach growled
in protest. She was starving. But she was also too
nervous to think about eating.

Glancing at the windows, she wondered how much someone on the outside could actually see in and worriedly asked Nick, ''Do you think a guard checks out the building at night?''

''For a small place like this? Not likely.''

''Then surely we won't be alone,'' she murmured as she stopped at a doorway and looked into the next room.

Empty.

''Looking for company?'' he asked.

''I thought the possibility of meeting up with some street kids was the idea of our being here.'' Otherwise, what was the point? They could have gone home and started out again the next day. ''I thought you wanted to stay someplace where Louise or someone who has seen her might show up.''

Then again, there was the possibility of running into someone dangerous. She fought her own disappointment that the building appeared truly deserted except for them and tried to stay positive.

''Right,'' Nick said. ''But you can't ever be sure who you'll find where.''

He seemed amused, which annoyed Isabel. There was nothing amusing about the situation—sleeping in some abandoned building, especially having agreed to improper conduct with him.

Improper Conduct. It sounded like a movie title. Or a courtroom charge imposed on her for having been such a bitch when she'd broken up with him.

This was it. Now she'd have to come through with her half of the bargain. She'd tried not to think about it too deeply all night, but now she had no choice.

They were alone and it was late. So exhausted that her eyes were getting heavy, she wasn't going to be able to stall for long or she would simply fall asleep, which might tick Nick off enough that he would leave her on her own.

She couldn't let that happen. She would have to give him the night of his life. *And of her own,* a little voice whispered. Isabel licked her lips and fought the edge of excitement that coursed through her at the thought of making love with the man again.

She remembered the first time. *Her* first time. Nick had been so gentle. So patient. So loving. Her heart ached for the innocents they had been then.

But neither of them had been innocent for years, not since her father's manipulation had sullied the love they'd once shared.

Think business, she told herself. Nothing personal. That was the only way she could get through the coming dark hours and live with herself afterward.

"I picked this particular place because I thought it would be safe," Nick said, wandering over to another door. "And because I figured the plumbing would still work."

"How considerate of you," Isabel mumbled, although she did actually appreciate the thought of a working toilet and running water, even if the water was cold. She hadn't really thought things through to that degree. "Where should we…uh…settle down for the night?"

Cleverly she was avoiding the word *sleep*. Somehow she doubted they'd be doing much of that, anyway.

"I picked the place. You pick the spot. Wherever you think you would be most comfortable."

"I'm not comfortable. I won't be until everything is resolved and Louise and I are reunited."

Not that a reunion would right things for either of them. But it would be a start.

"Could you make up your mind? I would like to eat before the food gets cold."

"Eat. Right," she muttered, tracing the area with the brilliant beam. As if she didn't have more important things on her mind. "How about over here?"

She'd indicated an inner room away from the street, while still being close to the toilet.

"Thank God," Nick muttered, finding what looked like a wooden packing crate behind the counter and carrying it into the smaller room.

Reluctantly, her pulse rushing a bit too loudly through her ears, Isabel followed.

In the center of the room, Nick was taking something out of the crate and turning the wooden box itself into a table, setting down the sack of food on its surface. Then he spread the blanket he'd removed before it.

"You want us to sit on that?"

"Better than the floor."

"But who knows where it's been?"

He shrugged. "Looks pretty clean to me."

Rather than argue, Isabel turned off her light and from the backpack pulled a few items she'd brought for the night. A clean sheet, a blowup pillow and a couple of votive candles, which she lit and placed on the crate.

"You certainly came prepared," Nick said as she spread the sheet over the blanket.

Physically, yes, she was prepared. Because deep inside, Isabel wasn't certain if she would ever be prepared for the situation she'd gotten herself into.

NICK'S EYES HAD ADJUSTED enough that he could see Isabel's jerky movements as she struggled with the edges of the sheet. He almost told her not to worry, that he'd left the blanket here earlier when he'd gotten the key to the lock from Nate, this being one of the buildings owned by Annie's paramour. But he didn't want Isabel to know he'd set things up to make living on the streets easier for her. He wanted her to learn something from the experience. He wanted her to know how he'd felt when he'd taken to the streets with nothing or no one—not even her—to come back to.

He wanted her to do something about it now.

But when he saw that Isabel was so uptight she looked ready to pop, he couldn't stand it.

"C'mon. Sit. Eat." *Forget about this blasted bargain you made,* he thought, though he couldn't put voice to the words. "You'll feel better with some food in you."

"I'll probably have heartburn."

"Always look at the bright side."

"There is no bright side to this situation," Isabel said.

"You'll change your tune when we find Louise."

"Will we?"

"If you had thought it would be easy, you wouldn't

have come to me,'' Nick said. He'd been thinking a lot about this—about what would happen now. He had to ask. ''Why did you come to me, Isabel?''

''You know why.''

''No, I really don't.''

And she didn't seem inclined to enlighten him. She sat a yard away, knees drawn up, arms wrapped tightly around her legs. The candlelight flickered, picked up silver highlights in her pale hair. She looked almost…innocent. And unhappy. He held out a soft-shelled taco wrapped in paper.

''Here, eat,'' he said, pushing it toward her.

Reluctantly, she took it and peeled back the paper. Then she took a tentative bite. ''Mmm, this is good.''

Nick grinned. The tacos were okay food, certainly not gourmet, but she was licking her lips as if they were the best thing she'd ever tasted.

She'd always had a deep appreciation for good food, he remembered, not like other high school girls who were always driving guys nuts counting calories. He'd liked that about her.

He'd liked so much about her.

He'd loved her….

Not wanting to recollect anything—not the little things that had once seemed so important, not the way he'd felt—he said, ''When you're hungry—really hungry, as in not having eaten for days—anything edible tastes heavenly.''

Mouth stuffed with the rest of the taco, she mumbled, ''Thank goodness we don't know what that's like, right?''

Nick avoided answering. Instead, he handed Isabel

another taco, which she attacked as greedily as the first. He watched her eat, mesmerized by the way she bit into the food, the shine of her lips and the way she darted out her tongue to get at the grease at the corner of her mouth.

The past intruded again, leaving him wondering how he could have been so wrong about her all those years ago.

Suddenly, he asked, "What is it you want out of life, Isabel?"

"What?" She swallowed her mouthful of food. "You're in the mood for a philosophical discussion?"

"I'm just wondering what kind of a person you've become."

What kind of a person she'd been all along. For the truth was, he hadn't known her at all.

She stopped eating and stared at him. "You mean, am I like my father? Yes, in some ways I am."

"You didn't have to tell me that. I found that out firsthand."

Her eyes widened. "That's not what I meant, Nick."

"What isn't?"

"The way I broke up with you. That is what you're referring to, right?"

"You think that's all I have on my mind?"

Her eyebrows drew together, and the nerves that had overtaken her before became apparent once more. "Now…considering the circumstances…maybe."

"What circumstances?"

"That we're going to…uh…that I'm going to… well, considering the deal we made and all."

Forget the damn deal. Be honest with me. That's all I want from you, he thought.

Now who was the liar? He wanted more all right, just not the way the cards had been dealt. In the end, he wouldn't go through with their bargain, wouldn't use her, even if she had once used him.

Nick knew who *he* was.

"All right," he finally said. "I admit I've given that last time we saw each other some thought."

Isabel sat very still. He imagined he could hear her struggle for breath. Imagined the glint in her eyes was not just candlelight but the sheen of unshed tears.

When she spoke, she did so in a whisper. "I'm sorry that I was so cruel."

Nick started. The last thing he'd expected was an apology. "Then why were you?"

He remembered that desperate night when he'd gone looking for her to tell her she wouldn't see him for a while. He'd found her with her friends and when he'd tried to get her aside, she'd laughed at him, told him that he'd been an experiment—that she'd wanted to know what the other half was like—and now she was bored with him. She'd not only driven him away, she'd driven a stake through his heart.

"Why, Isabel?"

"It doesn't matter."

"Of course it matters!"

"I said I was wrong. Isn't that enough for you?"

Enough for him? "No!"

"I did you a favor," she said, seeming unable to look at him. "We had no future together and I knew it. Hell, you knew it. I was only sixteen, too young for a serious relationship. And you were behind in school...."

"Which your father hated." Grayson had deemed him worthless without even knowing the circumstances. "I'm sure he talked me down every chance he got."

"Yes, my father did hate your being behind a year, just like he hated your disappearing acts. You can't blame him for not wanting his daughter to be with a boy he thought wasn't stable."

"Is that how *you* felt?"

Her gaze slid away from his. "You were ready to graduate," she continued, "and talking about not going on to college—"

"College isn't everything in life! Besides, you need money to go to college."

"Well, you got there somehow, didn't you?"

Staring at her perfect profile a moment, he finally said, "Eventually."

Someone with all the privileges in life had no idea what it had taken him to get there mentally. That had been the hardest part—believing in himself enough to get the education.

"But back then you would have stuck around just for me," she said softly.

"I loved you!" he grated.

"I'm sorry."

She was sorry? Because he'd really loved her or because of the way she'd ended things?

"It was for the best. I let you go the only way I could think of."

"You let me go? You drove me away!"

When he'd gone that night, he'd taken nothing with him but humiliation and heartbreak. He hadn't cared what happened to him, how he got along. He'd done things to survive that she would never understand.

He was a different man than he might have been.

And now she was trying to convince him that she'd destroyed him for his own good.

THE SUDDEN SILENCE CHILLED HER. Isabel felt the back of her throat thicken so that she could hardly swallow.

Somehow, rather than appeasing him with an apology, she had angered Nick in a way that she couldn't have anticipated. She felt it in his stare, in his body, which suddenly seemed stiff as a rock-hard wall, even from a distance. He was barely breathing, as if the air around her was tainted and he didn't want to be poisoned by it.

Needing an escape, if only for a few minutes, she said, "I, uh, need to use the facilities."

Flying to her feet, she grabbed her Maglite and whipped out of the room and to the toilet, where she closed the door for double privacy.

She'd slipped the cell phone in her pocket and meant to make that call to her father as promised. Flushing and turning on a faucet so that Nick wouldn't hear her, she punched out the number.

"It's me," she whispered when her father answered. "No Louise yet."

"Can you count on Novak?" he demanded.

"If anyone can find her, Nick can," she hedged, while wondering the same thing herself.

Once, she would have known the answer.

"How's Mother doing?"

"I would say that your mother is holding up better than one might expect. But then, Natalie has never allowed anyone to share her feelings."

Did that include him, her husband? Isabel wondered. She never had understood her parents' relationship, never remembered seeing affection between them. Cool civility was more like it. Unless they were before the cameras, of course. Then they were the consummate actors, playing at being a loving couple.

Isabel was mulling over the cause of their personal estrangement when her father asked, "By the way, where are you now?"

"Don't worry. I'm fine."

She gave him a few particulars about the search and agreed to report back to him the next day. Only after she hung up did she realize that, though she'd reassured him on her own, her father hadn't actually asked about her well-being.

Not that she was shocked. Or even surprised. As always, he simply assumed that she could take care of things—even herself.

But Isabel wasn't so sure of that. Not now. Not with Nicholas Novak, her Achilles' heel.

Why had she apologized to him? Why? And why had her apologizing made him so angry? She couldn't even imagine his reaction if she told him the whole truth.

And now she had to sleep with him.

Hating the position that her father had put her in... *no, be truthful, Isabel,* she told herself—the position she'd put *herself* in…she took a deep breath, opened the door and went to face the music.

Back in the makeshift bedroom, Nick looked at her through eyes that appeared to be dark pools in the candlelight. She felt devastated.

She couldn't stand it. She really couldn't. How the hell was she supposed to have sex with a man who seemed to hate her?

This was supposed to be a business deal. Nothing personal. At least no emotions involved. What had changed? Why was he looking at her like that and why did she feel as if she were going to explode?

Closing her eyes for a moment, Isabel gathered her energies to do what she had to.

Yet when she opened them and discovered Nick still staring at her, she found her voice was tight. "Aren't you going to get undressed?"

"I thought I would leave that to you."

"Will I have to pick you up and stand you on your feet so I can do it?"

He rose. "I'll take pity."

Would he? Isabel wasn't sure. When Nick stopped directly in front of her, she wanted to hit him for confusing her so.

And, just as much, she wanted to kiss him.

The thought suddenly appalled her. Kissing was too personal. Too emotional. She couldn't kiss him and then go through with it.

Instead, she pulled his T-shirt free of his jeans. Her fingers grazed his abs, rock hard, and he quickly sucked in his breath. She felt her pulse pick up.

"Do you have a lot of experience undressing men?" he asked.

"Enough."

"I imagine the others probably wear suits, though. And ties. And shirts with little buttons that—"

"Stop! Please." She pulled his T-shirt up, and he lifted his arms in compliance. Even so, she had to move closer to get the damn thing over his head. "Do we have to talk?" she choked out as her breasts brushed his now-naked chest. "Can't we just do this?"

Ripping the T-shirt free of him, she stood back and took a shaky breath.

He hesitated only a moment before saying, "I guess you really can."

Whatever that meant...

Thankfully, one of the candles had gone out, so she couldn't see him all that well. Doing it in the dark would help her remain dispassionate.

But undressing a man made it hard to be dispassionate, no matter how quick or clinical she tried to be. The sound of his zipper seemed to echo throughout the abandoned building and skitter up her spine. It was especially hard when in the midst of removing his briefs, he practically sprang into her hand. At the same moment, she heard a sound issue deep in his throat.

Her own breath caught as she surrounded him with fingers that trembled. He made another sound, but it was apparent that he was trying not to, was trying to hold back from enjoying this too much.

She took the challenge, though, slipped her hand

along his entire length with agonizing slowness until he groaned aloud. Her response was instantaneous. Her breasts tightened, the tips hardening and prodding the soft material binding them. And with each succeeding stroke to him, the sensation in her spread and deepened until her very center set on fire.

As if he knew it, as if he could smell her heat, Nick groaned and reached for her. He unsnapped and unzipped her jeans, dipped his hand inside and tested her through her panties, which quickly became damp against his fingers.

"You're ready," he whispered, tugging her jeans so they dropped to her ankles.

She thought he might take her there like that, but he dropped to the floor and removed her shoes and socks, then freed her of the jeans, all the while making love to her calves and the backs of her knees with his hands and fingers until her legs gave and she tumbled down next to him.

She knelt on the sheet and peeled off her T-shirt. He lay there, on his back, one knee slightly raised. She could barely see him, but flickers of candlelight showed her enough male flesh that she couldn't help but be aroused. She was only human, after all.

And, once upon a time, she had loved this man.

Closing her eyes, she touched him, starting at the knees and working her way up, now avoiding the part of him she would have to satisfy.

He touched her in return. His hand cupped her hip and moved lower until it hit her panties.

"You forgot something," he murmured.

"I didn't forget."

"You always did like to do things the hard way."

A reference to the past before they'd actually made love. She'd refused to take off her panties, so he'd first used his fingers and then his mouth on her through the material to make her come. Suddenly, just remembering, she felt trembly and a little faint.

And oh, so wet. The reminder and his hand still on her satin-covered flesh set off her hormones, stronger than any doubts or any sense of humiliation.

What she was feeling instead was hot and excited, and what she wanted was the satisfaction of knowing Nick as a man, allowing him to know her as a woman. They'd been little more than children before. Fumbling children who had learned about sensuality with each other. Now they had experience and the result of their making love could only be mind-blowing. She had no doubt.

A syrupy sensation flowed through her veins, and her woman's flesh throbbed for the feel of him hard and slipping against her.

She closed her eyes a moment and saw it. A close-up like he might do in one of his videos. She could visualize him, thick and dark and pulsing as he slid into her, burying his shaft to the hilt.

Taking a shaky breath, she leaned over and licked him, starting on his inner thigh, working past his cock and up his stomach. The warm, hard flesh that brushed her cheek jerked slightly and the wet heat between her own legs intensified.

She closed her mind to her prior objections, to un-fulfilled desires of the heart. She had needs gone unsatisfied for too long and she couldn't think of anyone she would rather be with to take care of them.

They were here.

He was hard.

She was ready.

They had a deal.

And she was going to take advantage of that for a night they would both remember.

Slipping out of her panties, she straddled him with her back to his front. Liquid pooled at her entrance as she rolled his head between the tips of her fingers and moved her bottom so that she spread herself over him.

His hands smoothed her naked buttocks and lightly kneaded her flesh, but other than that soft encouragement, he did nothing to force her. It was as if he was letting her make the final decision, not knowing, of course, that it was already made, that she had no choices. She couldn't stop herself if she wanted to. And she didn't want to.

With agonizing slowness, she braced her hands on his thighs and eased herself down on him, taking him inside her, inch by inch. He grunted and she felt him arch into her to go even deeper.

She remained poised with him buried inside, remembering the last time she'd been with him. *The first time she'd been with a man.* It had all been so different then. She had been madly, deeply in love.

Her heart palpitated, but she told herself it was the excitement, the hot drive of the moment.

Moving a hand off his thigh, she slipped it down under his penis and pulled up her bottom until her wet opening was barely covering his tip. Then she slid her fingers up and down his erection slick with her own moistness until the sensation forced him to move, to try to bury himself once more. He grasped her hips and rocked up into her until she lost her sense of control.

She simply rode him then, searching for that elusive state that would free her from the mounting tension.

"Let me," he urged, bringing his hand around her so that he inserted it between them.

With the first stroke against her clit, she left it to him, leaned forward once more and grabbed his thighs just above the knees. The pressure mounted rapidly, and she shuddered deep inside. She lost the last of her inhibitions. Freed of thought, she just wanted to come. Wanted to make *him* shout with pleasure. But the pace was out of her control.

It felt like a race to the finish—her riding him, him stroking her until, in a searing moment, her passion flared and she cried out only to hear his voice join hers, only to feel the gush of semen flood her as they came in tandem.

Isabel felt as if an emotional dam had burst in her, as well, and she was too enervated to do anything but let Nick pull her off him and onto the floor, where he tucked her into his side.

This almost felt right, she thought, curling a leg around his. Almost…if she didn't know better.

They'd had good sex, but that didn't mean anything. She'd made a deal, she reminded herself. And with that she'd have to be content. Still, she couldn't help but long for more even if she hadn't believed in fairy tales and happy endings for a very long time.

She couldn't help but pretend.

But as she lay in Nick's arms, listening to his breathing smooth out as he fell asleep, his face in her hair, an irony hit her.

Unlike the last time she'd been with Nick, in this situation she would have her father's wholehearted approval.

7

SENATOR WILLIAM GRAYSON stared out the bedroom window into the dark Chicago night as if he could divine where Louise was hiding out.

Damn the girl! If he couldn't stop her, she could ruin everything for him.

Deep in his gut he feared that some reporter would get to her before he did, and then a lifetime of hard work and devotion and sacrifice—yes, his sacrifice had been of the paramount sort—would be negated in a heartbeat. He hadn't ever meant for her world to be torn apart, but there it was. She hadn't been able to keep her nose out of what didn't concern her and now she would be sorry forever.

Guilt grazed his insides, but he brushed the unfamiliar sensation away.

Guilt was for the weak and he wasn't a weak man. The last thirty years were proof of that.

His chest squeezed painfully. He rubbed at it, then went to the highboy for the antacids in the top drawer.

Isabel would fix it, he assured himself as he chewed the temporary relief. He needed to keep calm. Isabel would fix things. Always had. He'd trained her well from the time she was a tot at his knee, wanting his attention. She would do anything for him, he reminded himself. Anything to win his love.

Besides, she was her mother's daughter, and if there was one thing her mother knew how to do, it was to put on a good face for the world.

"William, what are you doing up at this hour?"

"Worrying."

"Well, don't. Come to me and I'll make it all better."

"If only you could, Amber."

"All right, then I'll make it better for now."

Rising from the bed, she came to him and knelt before him.

Amber had always made him forget his troubles, even if only for now.

NICK AWOKE AT DAYLIGHT with Isabel tangled around him, sleeping soundly.

He lay still, afraid to move, afraid to touch this tempting woman until he got his morning hard-on under control.

But she was truly irresistible, with her full lips parted in sleep and her...

No, not again, he told himself. Three times in twice as many hours was enough. More than enough.

With her, he'd experienced some of the best sex that he'd ever had. *Ever.* But if he'd crazily thought sleeping with his first woman one more time would get her out of his system after all these years, he'd been sorely mistaken.

Moreover, though he didn't want to explore why

too closely, Nick recognized that while his body craved more, inside he wasn't feeling so good about the experience.

Disengaging his mind from the plush nude body pressed against his for the moment, he tried concentrating on the dance video he needed to start shooting for Club Undercover. But his idea of using images of the city at night only reminded him of Isabel.

Brightly lit towers transformed into pale silky hair whose shots of silver glinted against the dark night sky. The lake undulating in a lazy rhythm became her hips moving over him. And Buckingham Fountain with its shooting geyser made him think of his coming in her again.

Groaning, he chanced waking her by slipping out from under her limbs, but Isabel remained dead to the world as if she hadn't slept in days. Considering the depth of her concern for her sister, perhaps she hadn't.

And he'd taken advantage of that. Of her.

How could he have done it?

No matter which way he cut it, he'd used her, even after deciding he was better than that. Better than her father. Better than Isabel herself.

Was he really?

Even now, away from her, he had a hard-on that wouldn't quit. He wanted her now. He wanted her hard and fast. He wanted her soft and slow. He wanted her any way he could have her.

He was in pain from wanting her again, but he couldn't let her know that. Couldn't give her the advantage. She still had lessons to learn, but after last night undoubtedly she expected him to be putty in her hands.

The image that thought conjured made him groan yet again.

Too bad the place didn't come equipped with a shower. He could use a cold one. At least there was cold water of some kind, he thought gratefully, turning on the sink faucet. He ran his hands and arms under the stream, then ducked his head and doused his face, his neck, his hair, his chest. He kept dousing lower and lower until the chill got him under control.

What now? he wondered, knowing one look at her nude body would undoubtedly stir him all over again.

He would avoid looking at her. He would snatch up his clothes, dress, wait in the other room.

But he didn't have to worry about that. By the time he returned to their temporary quarters, she was up and dressed herself, her back turned to him as she zipped her jeans.

"Good morning," he murmured, staring at her derriere appreciatively, feeling the return of his erection.

"Morning."

She glanced back at him, started, whipped her head away again and hid behind a curtain of hair. So his nudity bothered her. He guessed she'd gotten more than she'd bargained for, even as he had.

"I'll be right back," she muttered, grabbing her backpack and leaving him standing there.

A moment later, he heard the water running. Was she just washing up or was she having to cool down just as he had? Doubtful. Isabel was the one who believed in expediency, he reminded himself.

By the time she returned, wearing a fresh T-shirt, her hair brushed and pulled back into a ponytail once more, he was dressed.

"What now?" she asked.

"We look for your sister."

"What about breakfast?"

"We could get coffee and some kind of breakfast sandwich at a fast-food place, I guess. But you'd better watch your money," he warned her. "When it's gone, it's gone."

"I have an ATM card!" she said sharply.

"Which you won't be using, not if you want my help."

After gaping for a moment, she said, "You certainly have a lot of rules."

"It's my game."

"Is that what Louise is to you—a game?"

"The hunt itself is a game, yes." At least the way he was making *her* play it. But he never took a person's safety lightly, especially not when that person was too young to fend for herself. But Isabel was a big girl now.

"Well, then I'd say you're one hell of a..." She took a deep breath and said, "Never mind. Let's get going."

Nick wondered what Isabel had been tempted to call him. Tyrant? Bastard? Prick? How could he blame her when she didn't know why he was torturing her? Undoubtedly, she assumed this was some sort of revenge, and maybe it was. But not in the way she thought.

WHY SHE STILL WANTED NICK, Isabel had no idea, but there it was. No matter how impossible he got with her at times, she took it. She tried to tell herself she was doing this for Louise.

Liar! her inner voice whispered. *You're doing this for yourself, because what happened between you and Nick was never settled.*

True enough. Her father had taken that opportunity from her. Only Nick had no clue about what had really happened. And she didn't know if she could ever tell him. If she could ever give him that power over her.

Not having had a real dinner the night before, she was starving. But heeding Nick's warning about doling out her remaining cash carefully, Isabel chose cheap. Her fast-food breakfast sandwich went down easier than she'd thought it might. And tasted better.

Sipping her coffee, she noted Nick checking out every person who came into the place.

"Looking for someone?"

"That's the idea, right?"

"You mean Louise—"

"Not specifically. Just someone who might have run into her."

Looking over the patrons herself, she asked, "How can you tell?"

"What?"

"A runaway."

"You can't always. Depends on how long they've been on the street."

"Why? What changes?" she asked. "What is it you actually see? Is it the clothes—"

"An edge. They're more alert to the minutiae around them. And more distrustful."

Isabel didn't want to go into the reasons. "But you don't see any in here."

He shook his head.

"Then maybe we ought to go where the chances are better."

Taking their coffees, they went to a local park. Another one. An empty one but for two women with baby strollers on the walkway.

Barely midmorning, the day was already hot.

Isabel threw herself on a bench in the shade of a big old tree and slugged down some coffee. "So be honest with me, Nick. Are we wasting our time?"

"You tell me." He stepped onto the bench and sat on the back of it, gazing around the park, ever alert. "We can quit whenever you say so."

"I don't want to quit. I want to find my sister."

"Then we're not wasting our time. But you're as impatient as ever."

"Me, impatient?"

"Remember the day you wanted to go swimming in the lake because it turned hot suddenly, and I told you that the water would still be too cold? You wouldn't listen."

"And I nearly froze to death." Remembering the incident at the start of their relationship, she laughed. Laughing felt good. She couldn't remember the last time something had truly amused her. "And you had to warm me up." Heat her up was more like it, she thought with a delicious shiver. "How was I supposed to know it would be so cold? It was June, for heaven's sake!''

"But we're talking about Lake Michigan.'' Nick raised his eyebrows at her. "And then there was the time you insisted on cutting your own hair because you just had to change your look *that* day and your stylist was on vacation.''

Isabel winced at that particular memory. "Ouch. That was a change, all right. I looked like a porcupine.''

"I thought you looked cute.''

Recognizing the soft tone that used to thrill her to her toes, a breathless Isabel insisted, "But I wanted to look sophisticated.''

She wanted to look that way for Nick, actually, she remembered. Nearly two years younger than he, she'd always been afraid that an older girl would turn his head.

"And then there was the time—''

"All right,'' she said with a laugh. "Enough, already. I get the picture. I've always been too impatient.''

Reminiscing about the old days softened her mood, though. She recollected whole days then when she'd been happy—when she'd been with Nick. In a strange way, she was happy now, just being with him, talking with him. It was almost as if all those years had never passed.

"On the other hand,'' Isabel said, "*you* were too relaxed. Nothing seemed to bother you.''

"Or maybe I was a good actor.''

Starting at his odd tone, she asked, "Were you acting, Nick? About everything?"

"You still don't trust me, do you?"

She hesitated only a second before hedging. "Still? What makes you think I didn't trust you?"

"Did you? Do you now?"

"Mmm." She made the inconclusive sound while sipping her now-cold coffee.

He shook his head. "If you trusted me, Isabel, you would tell me why Louise ran."

Back to that again. "What does *why* matter so much that you're stuck on it?"

He gave her a long, hard look before saying, "No reason, really. Just curiosity."

Despite his denial, the morning turned sour. And got hotter under his intense gaze. And Isabel's joke about taking a dip in the lake again didn't bring a smile back to Nick's lips.

Mouth suddenly dry, not knowing how to relieve the tension, Isabel was about to suggest they get going when her backpack started ringing.

Hands shaking, she ripped into it in search of the cell phone. Her father wouldn't call unless it was an emergency, and few other people had the number because the phone was so new. But Louise was one of those people, she thought, unable to get the damn phone unfolded fast enough. A quick glance at her caller ID showed a number that she didn't recognize.

"Hello!" she said breathlessly, her gaze locking with Nick's.

"Is this Izzie?" came a young, unfamiliar female voice.

Her heart raced. Only one person used that wretched nickname. "Speaking."

"This is Angela from the Runaway Switchboard."

"Runaway Switchboard?" she echoed, and Nick slid down on the bench next to her.

"Part of our mission is to pass on messages from runaway kids to family or friends."

Snugged up to her side now, Nick pressed his head to hers, and Isabel ignored the immediate flush that went through her. Obviously he wanted to hear, too, so she tilted the phone from her ear slightly.

"Did Louise, um, Lulu ask you to call?"

"She did," Angela said. "She wanted you to know that she's all right."

"Where is she now?"

"I'm sorry, but I don't have that information. I only pass on what I'm asked to."

Not wanting to let go of this link to her sister, Isabel asked, "Did she say when she was coming home? Or that she wanted to see me elsewhere?"

"Let me read her message," Angela said. "'Izzie, I love you. Don't try to find me, because knowing what I do about Daddy, I can't live in that house anymore. But you don't have to worry about me. I'm safe. Lulu.'"

Safe—what did that mean? A place to stay? People to take care of her?

"When did Lulu call?"

"Just a few minutes ago. I took the call myself. I got you on the first try."

A few minutes ago. Thank God she was all right, at least for the moment.

"Can I give you a message to pass on to her?" Isabel asked.

"I can't guarantee she'll actually get it. She would have to call in. But I can take it. Hang on—I'm setting it up on the computer." A light click of keys was followed by "If you want, you can give it to me as if you're talking to your sister and I'll enter it exactly that way. Okay, go ahead."

Pulse threading unevenly, Isabel said, "Lulu, I'll do whatever you need so that you'll come home. We can get our own apartment. I'll make a new home just for the two of us if that's what would make you happy."

Angela asked, "Is that it?"

"Please add 'I love and miss you. Izzie.'"

"Got it."

As the young woman disconnected, Isabel locked in the number of the hotline on her caller ID just in case she needed to use it later.

And then she sat on the bench, too stunned to move. The contact with her sister hadn't been as direct as she'd hoped for, but it was something. At least for the moment, she knew Louise was alive and well.

Perversely she now felt like crying.

And, as if he knew how she was feeling, Nick rubbed her shoulder and then pulled her closer into his side. She'd been so tense that she hadn't even realized he'd wrapped his arm around her. Now she collapsed against him and let go of a strangled sob.

"Go ahead and cry if you want," Nick murmured, stroking her hair gently. "You don't have to be tough all the time."

She let go, but only for a moment. Then with a hiccup, she brought herself back under control.

"I've cried enough," she said, choking back her emotions. "Crying doesn't get you what you want or need." She squeezed her eyes against the tears that threatened, anyway. "Crying won't bring my sister home."

"That sounds like the senator speaking."

His observation was softened by the arm around her, by the hand stroking her arm, making her heart and her body quicken in response.

"As you noted before," she said, "we are a lot alike."

"Then maybe you need to cut loose, too. Getting a place for you and your sister might do you both good."

Even though she'd been the one to suggest it in her message to Louise, Nick's bringing it up irritated Isabel. Certain he'd heard her sister's message, he now knew Louise's running had something to do with their father, something that was more than a simple fight. Any inclination to weep now swept away, she pushed away from him before he could renew that particular topic.

"What is your hang-up about my living in the family home?" she demanded. "It wasn't long after I graduated from college that Father got elected to the Senate, and I certainly wasn't ready to move out then. And since then, he hasn't spent but a few months out of each year here in Chicago. More important, Louise tried school in D.C. for a semester but hated it. She wanted to come back, to live with me here and go to her old school, so my staying in the town house is a perfect arrangement for everyone.''

''I'll bet it is. The senator has you all tied up twenty-four/seven.''

Why did he keep harping on her relationship with her father? Isabel wondered.

''Just because your father walked out on you and your mother when you were a kid—and you always said you didn't care—doesn't mean that other people don't want lasting relationships with *their* parents!''

In amazement, she watched Nick close her off as surely as if a curtain had come down between them. He turned his back on her and began walking.

He could criticize her and her father all he wanted, but let her just mention his...

Slinging her backpack in place, she rushed after him before he could lose her.

KNOWING WHAT I DO ABOUT DADDY...

What had Louise meant by that? Nick wondered.

I can't live in that house anymore.

Nick knew Louise's running had something to do with the senator, something that went beyond a simple argument over her teenage quirks. That had been apparent from the first.

Whatever it was, Isabel wouldn't let him in on the scoop. Instead she'd used some dark truths about his own past to distract him.

Of course, she didn't know the whole truth about him, either, and he wasn't about to be any more forthcoming than she. Besides, what had happened to him was ancient history.

Just as *they* were ancient history, he thought regretfully.

Knowing what I do about Daddy... Louise's words echoed through his mind.

She felt betrayed. He understood that feeling. Disgusted. That one, too. Only what exactly had gotten to her? Had the betrayal been public or personal?

Considering Louise was only seventeen, Nick suspected it would have to be personal.

Why couldn't her message have been a little more direct?

What the hell could Senator William Grayson have done to drive his teenage daughter from her own home?

WHEN THEY STOPPED TO COOL DOWN and relax for a while at Helen's Cybercafé midway through the afternoon, Isabel took refuge from Nick in the bathroom, which offered a multitude of pleasures as far as she was concerned.

She would take a sorely needed break from the renewed tension between them. She would refresh herself, wash off some of the sweat and city grime. What was really called for was a full shower—as if he would let her go somewhere to take one. While here, she also planned to get hold of her father and demand an answer to the big question Louise's message had raised in her mind.

To that end, she retrieved her cell phone and placed the call to his office, all the while rehearsing how she would approach it. When he wanted to be, her father could be an impenetrable wall.

"McNulty here."

"Hey, Danny, it's Isabel. I need to speak to my father."

"Sorry, Isabel, the senator had an appointment outside the office. He didn't say when he'd be back."

Jeff Enger's assistant wasn't exactly in the loop, Isabel knew, thinking it odd that he was in her father's office alone. Now what?

"Hey, is this about Louise?" Danny asked.

"Sort of, yes."

His buoyant tone flattened when he asked, "Then you didn't find her?"

"Not yet, though I have some hopes for tonight. That's what I wanted to tell my father." At least it was part of what she wanted to talk to him about. "Maybe you can give him a message for me."

"Sure thing. I have a pad and I'm already writing. So you might be able to find Louise later...."

"Maybe. She was seen at a place called Club Undercover the other night. The staff will be watching for her, and the owner will call me if anyone spots her."

And she and Nick had agreed to canvas the vicinity—just in case she popped up at Eye-Candy or one of the local cafés. It was about the only thing they *had* agreed on.

"Maybe this will be it, then," Danny murmured so softly that she had to strain to hear. "We can only hope."

"Right," Isabel agreed. "We can hope."

Finding Louise would just be the beginning of the battle. Then she would have to overcome her sister's objections, whatever they might be, and talk her into coming home. Or at least to someplace where Isabel could keep her safe.

Frustrated that she hadn't been able to talk to her father and quiz him about Louise's message, she said, "Danny, would you add something to that missive? Ask my father to call me. Tell him that it's important, that there's something Louise said to me that I need him to explain."

Silence at the other end.

"Danny?"

"Yeah, yeah, I'm here. Just writing," he said. "Anything I can help you with?"

"No. I mean, thanks, but my father is the one who needs to do the talking."

The question was—would he?

8

NICK FINISHED CHECKING his e-mail and logged out. Thankfully, the messages had been personal—nothing professional he had to deal with just yet. He was relieved that Isabel had not yet come out of the bathroom to see him at the computer. With all the rules he'd imposed on her, she would undoubtedly accuse him of cheating.

And, of course, she would be right. He didn't know too many runaways with access to e-mail.

About to get his coffee, he saw Helen coming around the counter, a cup in each hand.

"For you and your lady," she said, setting them at a table.

"I told you—"

"I know what you told me." Helen slid into a chair. "But I trust my eyes more than empty words. You still have a thing for her, bucko."

"And you have a great imagination," he hedged, sitting opposite Helen.

"Do I? She looked exhausted when you two dragged in here. And you looked pretty pleased with yourself. It seems to me you're putting her through her paces. And you're doing that because you don't care anything about her?"

"I just want her to know what's it like to be a scared kid on the run without many resources. Well, as much as she *can* know, since she has backup. She can always go home or use her ATM card as she threatened to do," he said in disgust.

Helen's green eyes widened. "Fascinating."

"What is?"

"How bad you've got it. Nick Novak, the original one-night stand, is hammered! What the heck did she do to you, anyway, that she's got you so tied up in knots?"

Before he had to come up with some bogus answer to appease his nosy friend, he spotted Isabel cutting across the café.

So all he said was "I want her to get something out of this experience, Helen. I want her to do something to cut away at the problem." And as Isabel drew closer, he added, "And here she is now."

Isabel frowned. "Were you two talking about me?"

"Just wondering what was taking you so long," Nick said.

"I was enjoying the running water. The *warm* running water." Sitting next to him, she muttered, "But I would enjoy a shower a whole lot more."

"Sorry, can't help you there," Helen said with a smile. "But I can offer you coffee as a pick-me-up."

"Thanks." Isabel picked up the cup and grinned at her.

And Nick felt his gut tighten.

For a moment, she reminded him of the old Isabel. The one who used to let down her guard only with him. He'd seen that in her earlier in the park when they'd laughed over old times, and here it was again with Helen. He wondered how often she had a reason to laugh, to relax, to be the Isabel she could be when not under her father's influence. Not often enough, he was certain.

And when she learned what he'd been hiding from her, would she ever smile that way at him again?

"DEATH IS PRECIOUS...death wraps its arms around us...death is the ultimate fantasy..."

The things he had to put up with to find the little bitch!

An undulating sea of teenagers, some sitting, some standing on the dance floor crowding the stage, bobbed their heads as the young poetess dressed in black made dire predictions while he tried to gain entrance to Club Undercover, thanks to the lead Isabel had so thoughtfully provided with her phone call.

"Excuse me, sir," the purple-haired hostess said, stepping in front of him. "This is one of our early teen nights. We don't serve alcohol until after ten."

"No problem, it's not a drink I'm looking for."

The hostess frowned at him and he figured she was winding up to object to his going in, maybe thinking he liked little girls.

Yeah, right. If she only had a clue about his true intentions.

But forcing a smile, he said, "Listen, I'm just looking for my cousin's daughter. She sat for my kids yesterday and now the little one's Binky is missing— a stuffed bunny with floppy ears," he explained. "He drove me crazy crying for it, kept me up all night. I thought she might know where it is. The kid will never get to sleep without the damn Binky.'' Seeing the hostess was almost convinced that he was telling the truth, he added, ''Look, if you need ID or something...''

''No, of course not. Go ahead.''

Smooth, he thought as she stepped aside and he sidled in looking for Louise.

He edged around the dance floor and kept his focus shifting for the brat. It wasn't until he was nearly around the room that he looked back and spotted her coming in. Another girl with bright red hair waved Louise over.

''I rise, my wings spread...'' the poetess went on as he backed off and found a seat ''...and I soar toward the light...only to be engulfed...in its flames!''

He watched Louise's friend shove a glass of what looked like cola at her. She sat there, pretending interest in the performance. And though she fingered the rim of the glass, she didn't pick it up to drink.

He'd never seen her look so unhappy, and just for a moment, he pitied her. She was only a kid who knew too much.

But the last was the important part that he needed to keep in mind. And pity would only confuse the issue.

Trying to decide what to do now, he saw his opportunity when the girl onstage stopped, the audience applauded, and Louise rose and threaded her way toward the rest rooms.

He sauntered after her to the area off to one side

of the club. By the time she exited the ladies' room a few minutes later, he was so tense he was ready to pop a few of those pills burning a hole in his pocket.

He didn't need the pills, he told himself.

Hooking the brat under the arm, he spoke close to her ear. "Come over here with me, Louise. We need to talk."

Clearly shocked that he'd caught up to her, she let herself be pulled farther from the noise. And witnesses.

"What are *you* doing here?" she demanded to know.

"Trying to talk some sense into you."

"I have nothing to say to you…you…you liar!"

"Look, things don't have to be like this. Promise you won't tell anyone what you know and everything will be okay."

"Just leave me alone or you'll be sorry."

"Is that a threat? 'Cause if that's a threat, I can make one of my own—"

"Isabel won't let you hurt me!" Louise spat out in a low, angry tone. "I could tell whoever I want. You can't do anything to us."

He gripped her arm tighter. "I can take care of two as easily as one."

"Let go!" she shrilled, jerking her arm, ineffectually trying to free herself. "Or the whole world is going to know about you!"

"Is there a problem?" a dark-haired young waiter asked.

"No, no problem," he said, letting Louise go.

That's all it took. Before he could stop her, she'd

darted through the crowd and headed for the exit. He tried following but got tangled up in the noisy melee. Louise was fast and knew better than he how to maneuver through this crowd. She put too much distance between them for him to catch up.

He was still struggling to get loose of the crowd when he saw her fly out the entrance and start up the stairs.

Damn it!

She knew too much and she wouldn't keep what she knew to herself forever. Young and hotheaded, she spoke before she thought. And when she spoke to the wrong person and the shit hit the media, everything would be ruined.

He couldn't let that happen, not after the waiting game he'd been playing. He couldn't let her talk.

Couldn't let her live, really, he decided dispassionately.

Then, once he got rid of his biggest liability, he would be forced to reconsider Isabel and what *she* might do with what she knew. Or thought she knew, he amended, because she didn't have the whole picture, not without a heart-to-heart with the brat.

Being an admitted political creature of the worst sort, he would do what he must, even if that meant ridding his world of *both* sisters.

HAVING GOTTEN A CALL from Gideon that one of his employees had spotted Louise, Isabel rushed down the stairs into Club Undercover, Nick at her heels. Leaving her backpack behind the hostess's stand, she stopped just inside the entrance, her gaze sweeping over the young customers who populated the space. On stage, two teenagers in white face were miming a romantic tryst, and members of the audience were hooting and calling out dialogue for them.

"Do you see her?"

"No. But it's difficult to see anyone up there," she said, indicating the tables and booths that rose several levels above them.

"So what are we waiting for?" Nick asked, starting up one side of the raised seating area.

Isabel followed and got a closer look at every teenager in the house.

No Louise.

When they went full circle and ended up back on the main level, Nick asked, "Now what?"

Taking one last look around, she froze and gripped his arm. "Rosalyn!" she said. "Louise's best friend. The girl who lives in this neighborhood and who Louise went to see. Over there."

As quickly as the crowd would let them pass, they crossed to the table where the redhead's focus was on a cute boy with curly blond hair. The redhead turned, and as she connected with Isabel, her eyes widened and her sappy lovesick smile faded.

"Isabel, hi."

"We need to talk away from the noise."

Sighing, the girl whispered something in her date's ear, then got up and moved toward the entrance.

Isabel barely waited until she'd stepped foot in the club's foyer before she turned on the redhead. "Okay, Rosalyn, start talking!" Used to dealing with her own teenage sister, she took on the same stern persona that she sometimes had to with Louise. "You said you didn't know where my sister was, but people saw you together tonight."

Sometimes a stretch of the truth went a long way. The bluff worked. Rosalyn visibly caved.

"All right, I did see her," the girl admitted, "but only for a few minutes. I don't know where she is now, honest. Lulu called me earlier and said she needed to see me."

"So she met you here like she wanted. What did she tell you?"

"Tell me?" Rosalyn's forehead creased in a frown. "I don't get it."

So Rosalyn didn't know, which probably meant Louise hadn't told anyone.

Relieved that she didn't have the situation with her father to deal with just yet, Isabel said, "I just was wondering what you talked about."

"Not about where she was staying if that's what you mean," Rosalyn assured her. "We didn't even have time to talk. She said she had to go to the ladies' room and the next thing I know I see her running out the door."

Isabel started. "Running? Why?"

The girl shrugged. "I, uh, was kind of busy. I just figured she wanted to leave, is all. That was maybe ten minutes ago."

"I missed my sister by a mere ten minutes." The breath whooshed out of her. "Oh, my God."

Nick put an arm around Isabel and steadied her. "Are you sure she won't be back?" he asked Rosalyn.

"I don't know!" The girl drew herself together. "Look, I don't know why she left or where she went or if she'll be back. I'm going back to my date before he finds himself a new girl!"

Isabel freed herself of Nick's support and stopped her from escaping. "Rosalyn, wait. I'm sorry I came on so strong, but you must know I'm sick with worry about Louise."

The girl softened her stance. "I told her to go home, honest, Isabel, but I don't think she will. If she calls again, I—I'll see if I can find out where she's holed up."

"Thank you."

If she has a place to stay.

Isabel closed her eyes against the thought, and once more felt Nick's hand on her shoulder.

Isabel opened her eyes. Rather than running back to her date, Rosalyn was still standing there, wavering.

"I, um, was thinking...it didn't occur to me before, but we used to hang out at this place and pretend we were alone on an adventure. We'd tell each other wild stories. Once last year when Lulu got in trouble with your dad, she threatened to run away and hide there until he was sorry he was so mean."

"Where?"

"About a mile from here in Bucktown, on the incline by the railroad tracks, there's this little storage shed. At least there used to be. I don't even know if it's still there with all the new construction going on."

She explained how to find the opening and how to

get up the incline that led to it. The railroad was pretty well inaccessible or fenced off to keep vagrants—or kids—from walking along the tracks that were raised fifteen or twenty feet above street level.

"We'll check it out, Rosalyn. Thanks," Nick said.

"Really," Isabel added. "Thank you."

No sooner had the girl left them than Isabel turned to Nick. "A lousy ten minutes. Can you believe it?" She stepped into his arms as if it were the most natural thing in the world. "She must have been leaving just as Gideon called."

His arms encircled her, and Isabel had to steel herself so that she didn't cry. They had another place to check, so there was reason to hope. Still, she stayed put just for a moment, remembering Nick holding her like this in the old days, after she'd fought with her father about seeing him.

Emotions high, she wished they were somewhere private, somewhere she could lose herself in him as she had the night before. Even now, even when the pain of not knowing if she would be reunited with Louise was so sharp, she wanted Nick, and it was more than business for her. She could pretend all she liked, but the truth was, she needed him for more than finding her sister.

Unsure of how long they stood like that, her trembling against Nick's rock-solid strength, him supporting her as if he actually cared, she gradually became aware of Gideon's presence. From the way Nick stiffened slightly, he did, too.

"I'm sorry," Gideon said to Isabel. "If I could have detained your sister and locked her in my office without bringing the authorities down on me, I would have.''

Tearing herself out of Nick's embrace, Isabel wrapped her arms around herself, as if she could choke away the longings that suddenly threatened to consume her.

''You couldn't have done that,'' she told the club owner. ''Louise wouldn't have gone quietly.''

Isabel took a normal breath with difficulty. Everything was becoming too much for her. Losing Louise had been tough enough on her emotions. Finding Nick had made things worse. Now she felt as if she were teetering on a tightrope without a safety net.

''Come into my office,'' Gideon suggested. ''Maybe I can figure out what happened.'' He stopped to speak to Mags. Isabel heard him saying, ''Ask the staff if anyone saw anything going on with the girl.''

Mags repeated the request over the mike attached to the earphones that she and the wait staff all wore.

By the time they got into his office, the telephone was ringing. Gideon answered and listened a moment. Then he said, ''Okay, send him in here,'' and hung up. He turned to them. ''A waiter named Todd saw Louise arguing with a man.''

When Todd entered the office and was questioned about the encounter, however, he wasn't able to offer them anything in the way of a description.

''I mean, it's real dark back there and the guy's clothes were black and he wore a billed cap pulled low,'' Todd said. ''I barely saw him for a second.''

''Did you hear anything he said?'' Nick asked.

''Kind of a jumble—it was noisy like always.

Something about a threat and taking care of two as easily as one…and then I heard the girl tell him to let go. He was holding on to her until I asked if there was a problem. He said no and when he let her arm go, she took off fast.''

Gideon asked, ''Didn't you realize this was the girl you were supposed to be watching for?''

An uncomfortable Todd glanced at his boss. ''Sorry. I was late tonight. No one brought me up to speed.''

The club owner turned to Isabel. ''Whatever happened, it doesn't sound like your sister will be back, not tonight.''

She sighed. There was the shed, if it still existed. That was worth a try.

''But you have tomorrow night, too,'' Gideon said. ''Louise obviously likes places like this—with entertainment and lots of her contemporaries hanging out.''

''That would only make sense, her gravitating to places that would make her comfortable. Louise was always a social girl,'' Isabel admitted. ''And she's into music.''

''There's going to be a rave a few miles from here,'' Gideon said, ''just west of the Loop.''

''Rave?'' Isabel echoed. ''An illegal party?'' Illegal because unlicensed ''businesses'' moved from place to place operating these raves, and the parties were known to be hotbeds for drug activity. ''I don't think Louise would go for that.''

''Just in case…'' Gideon scribbled something on a

pad and ripped off the top sheet of paper "...here's the address."

They thanked him and left, and Isabel retrieved her backpack from Mags.

All the while her worry over Louise deepened. A rave. While she hoped not, she just wasn't certain anymore what her sister would or would not do.

When they got back outside, the walkway in front of the club was packed with more than a dozen raucous teens. Nick led them along the curb around a flirting couple and guys who were goofing around, jostling each other in a mock fight.

Beyond the parked cars, vehicles whizzed along Milwaukee. Isabel slowed down, suddenly feeling spooked.

"A cold front is coming in," Nick was saying as the distance between them grew.

But Isabel was only half listening. She shivered, but whether from a change in temperature or her prickling instincts, she wasn't certain.

Something was off.

Stopping at the curb, she felt as if she was being watched. Louise? Was her sister somewhere nearby? Isabel wondered hopefully. She concentrated...scanned the area on the other side of Milwaukee...thought maybe she saw a girl with long blond hair duck into an entryway.

Balanced on the curb, she looked for Nick to tell him she was going to cross and check it out. A sharp shove from behind knocked the backpack from her grip and sent her flying out past the parked cars. She pitched forward, off balance, and landed in the street on both hands and knees.

Shaken, she looked up as the headlights of a fast-moving vehicle headed straight at her.

9

AN EAR-PIERCING SHRIEK made Nick look back in time to see Isabel fly into the street. Its headlights holding her in shock, an SUV ate pavement fast. Nick's heart froze in his chest as he fought the crowd to get to her.

With a screech of brakes, the SUV jerked to a stop mere inches from running her over, and Nick felt the relief like a physical blow.

"What the hell do you think you're doing, bitch?" the driver yelled from his open window.

Nick cut through milling bodies and got to Isabel's side. He helped her to her feet and concentrated on her welfare rather than dragging the jerk out of his yuppie wagon and shoving those words back down his throat like he wanted to do.

Taking her in his arms, he held her close. For a moment, at least, she clung to him like a lifeline. And Nick realized he wanted her to do that. No matter how she'd treated him in the past, he still had feelings for her. Maybe he was crazy, but he wanted to be there for her in every sense of the word.

If she had been hurt...

A couple of curious kids drew closer, whether to see that she was all right or to get a good seat for some exchange of hostilities, Nick didn't know. Other drivers in vehicles behind the SUV—obviously not attuned to what was holding up traffic—leaned on their horns while Nick, his arm still around her, helped Isabel limp back to the sidewalk.

The SUV took off with an audible tear of rubber.

"You okay?" a girl they passed asked.

The kids were all concentrating on them now.

"Yeah, fine, thanks," Isabel said.

She didn't sound fine, Nick thought, and how could she be after that scare? His own pulse was jagging as if he'd run a marathon.

"You want to go back inside?" he asked.

"No." Though she still seemed dazed, Isabel looked all around them. "I'm fine. Just shaken up. I want to get away from here. But my backpack..."

"I'll check." Reluctantly, Nick let her go and stepped away for a moment to look for it. "Not here. Did anyone see a backpack?"

Answering murmurs were all negative, and several of the teens moved off.

He returned to Isabel's side. "It's...um...gone."

"Like L-Louise."

He realized she might be dazed, but she was checking out the kids still there as though she would spot her sister if she looked hard enough. He took her in his arms again and lightly held her against his chest.

"Louise isn't here, Isabel," he murmured into her hair. "And neither are your things."

"I don't c-care about things."

Shock was setting in. And so was the cold front that had brought the temperature down a good ten degrees or so. She was shivering against him, Nick realized. If it got any cooler or rained like predicted, their search would be called to a halt.

"Let's go somewhere to get a drink," he suggested.

Pushing herself away from him, she said, "I don't need a drink."

Now she was sounding peevish. She needed to sit and calm down. "Well, *I* need a drink," he insisted. "A double."

Taking her hand, Nick led Isabel down the block to a neighborhood restaurant with a pleasant bar he liked. Not a fancy place, it was cozy and dark and decorated with tiny white Christmas lights all year round. A booth in the corner was empty, so he commandeered it, ordered Isabel to sit and fetched two double brandies from the bar.

Isabel remained quiet long enough that Nick was starting to worry about her. He watched her hand tremble as she lifted the brandy to her lips. And his eyes widened when, rather than taking a small sip, she gulped the whole drink.

"Oh," she murmured as she set down the empty glass next to a lit candle. Her eyes widened, as well. "That's better."

"At least you know you're still alive."

"If bruised and grubby and missing my backpack."

Her lifeline, he thought. "So the flashlight is gone. And the cell phone."

"Actually, the Maglite is clipped to a loop on my jeans." She showed him. "And the cell phone is in my pocket—luckily, I've had it there all day—and my wallet is in the other pocket.''

"Then you're down to the basics. But you don't have anything to worry about," Nick said, "unless you had another clean T-shirt stashed in that bag."

"Among other things."

"Unmentionables?"

She stared at him suspiciously. "Knowing you, you'd like me to mention them."

"Thoroughly and often."

The teasing brought a tentative smile to her lips.

"Another drink?" he asked.

"Give this one a minute to kick in."

The dim light suited Isabel. It softened her. Or maybe that was simply the brandy already kicking in. She was relaxing before his eyes. So beautiful. So soft. No, the last was an illusion, he reminded himself.

He didn't know another woman who could be harder when she needed to be. Or one more talented at being whatever she deemed necessary for the situation.

Was that what she was doing now?

Somehow, Nick didn't think so. More and more, he felt she was showing her true self to him. And rather than being a bonus, that made *him* uncomfortable. It made him think of her as a real flesh-and-blood woman—one he cared about. It made him think that what they were doing was questionable—or, rather, what he'd let her do the night before.

"Where did you learn to drink like that?" he asked, trying to get his mind around his growing guilt.

"I hang around with politicians, remember. Deals don't always get made in official places."

Nick took a swig of his own drink. "And that's okay with you?"

Isabel sighed and looked at him as though he were too naive for words. "It's reality, Nick. It's been that way for, oh, centuries? Isn't that the way the rest of the world works—contracts made through networking? For instance, your deal with Gideon. How did that come about?"

Remembering he'd met Gideon at the club bar, Nick caved. "Okay, you have a point." He saluted her and took another sip of the brandy. Mellowing himself, he asked, "So what the hell happened out there on the street? Did you miss the curb? Or trip?"

"Neither. I was pushed."

He swore under his breath. "One of those guys horsing around must have bumped into you."

"No, not bumped. *Pushed.*"

That took him aback. "You mean...purposely?"

"I felt hands in the middle of my back, Nick. Yes, I mean purposely."

So that was the reason she'd been checking out the crowd so thoroughly after he'd helped her up. And here he'd thought she'd simply been looking for her sister.

"What the hell?" he murmured.

"You can say that again."

"Why would some kid try to hurt someone he didn't know?" Nick frowned, trying to remember if he saw anyone who'd looked suspicious. No, he'd been concentrating on her. "Unless he was high on something."

"Right. He was probably high," she agreed.

But the simple conclusion left him uneasy. Left him wondering if there was another explanation. A connection to their being followed the night before.

Nick didn't want to believe it, but he was beginning to suspect someone might be after Isabel herself.

ANOTHER BRANDY LATER, Isabel felt as if she'd been lit by a torch inside. She was relaxed, almost happy... except for the moments when Louise crossed her mind.

"So, Nick, tell me about you," she demanded. If she kept him talking, she wouldn't have to think for a while and she surely could use a break from worrying. Besides, fair was fair. He'd wanted to know about her—not that she'd given him much—so it was his turn to talk. "What is it *you* want out of life?"

"Getting philosophical?"

Isabel started when he turned her own words back against her. Turnabout was fair play, she guessed. "More like curious about the real you."

"I want the same thing as everyone—to be happy."

"Are you?"

"Sometimes."

She fiddled with the brandy glass, watched the small pool of amber liquid slide across the bottom. "Like when?"

"When I do something that gives my life meaning."

"Like making your documentary on the runaway teenagers."

"There's that," he agreed.

Again, Isabel thought about following his lead. The past twenty-four hours had been a real eye-opener. She'd barely had a taste, but she was beginning to understand how bad it could be, especially for kids who weren't prepared to take care of themselves.

Life on the Streets.

She could see it now. An article. A feature in the *Sunday Tribune Magazine,* perhaps. She needed a personal angle. Not her sister, though. She would never use Louise like that. But what would be wrong with using the things *she* was actually experiencing?

A firsthand account…hmm.

"Where did you go?"

Realizing Nick was waving a hand in front of her face, she came to with a start. "Oh, sorry. I was just thinking." Not wanting him to ask about what until she had it figured out—she didn't want him laughing at her—she said, "So, what else makes you happy?"

A strange expression flicked through his features. "I take things day to day and try to find something, even a small thing, to appreciate."

Why did she get the feeling that one of those things included being with her? Throat tight, she asked, "As in?"

"Sitting on that park bench earlier today. Laughing with you."

He did mean her!

Had things changed in Nick's mind? Isabel was certain that he hadn't wanted to help her. That he'd only agreed with stipulations because he wanted to get even.

"Simple things," she murmured.

"I'm a simple guy."

"Liar." Nick Novak was perhaps the most complex man she'd ever known—and, despite that she called him a liar, probably the most honest. "Just because you're not into making money—"

"Ah, there it is!" he said, leaning forward so the table candle distorted his face with shadows and light.

"There? What?"

"The money god. I can't forget how important a big bank account is to you."

"Says who?"

"Wasn't my poverty and low-class existence the reason you broke up with me?"

A pulse beat in her throat. "Not exactly."

"What exactly, then?"

Tempted to tell Nick the truth, Isabel couldn't give him the motivation to go after her father, not now. Especially not with an election coming up and the Senate seat on the line. And, considering what Nick had required her to do in exchange for his cooperation, she knew he was capable of anything.

"We're supposed to be talking about you, not the past," she reminded him, trying to turn the conversation back to a safer topic.

"The past *is* about me."

"I would rather have a look into your future."

"I'm never going to be rich," he predicted.

Money, again. He certainly was hung up on the subject.

"What about having a place to call home?" she asked. "Is that in your future?"

"Not immediate. I'm in no hurry to burden myself with a house or condo and all the trappings that go with ownership."

"You could rent a nice apartment and get a roommate," she suggested.

"In case you forget, I don't play well with others."

"You play very well when you want to," Isabel murmured, once again remembering things better left forgotten.

How he'd charmed her.

How he'd seduced her.

How she'd broken his heart.

She thought he remembered, too. The way he was looking at her—with hunger in his eyes—made her think his mind was on what they shared before her betrayal. Her pulse rushed and her cheeks flared with heat. That longing she'd tried to ignore stretched toward him with invisible arms.

"Aren't you ever lonely?" she asked softly.

"I have friends."

That wasn't what she wanted to know. Of course he had friends. Nick always had friends. Probably good friends he would go the distance for, and vice versa. But how well did he let them know him? Who did he let in and how far?

Somehow, Isabel didn't think he'd changed in that respect. He'd kept a side of himself buried deep, but she'd always known it existed. He simply hadn't trusted her enough to show it to her. And considering the way things had turned out, perhaps that had been for the best. But how sad if he couldn't be open with anyone.

Just the way she couldn't.

The comparison gave her a rush that felt like a real connection. Some things they had in common—mistrust and secrets. What a great way to build a relationship!

Isabel reminded herself that's not what she was doing with Nick. Once they found Louise, she had no idea if she would ever see him again. The thought left a lump in her stomach and a renewed warning to keep her emotional distance.

Shoving the brandy glass away from her, she said, "Well, I'm ready."

He raised an eyebrow and repeated, "Ready?"

Determined not to let him bait her, she kept her voice even. "To check out the shed."

"Oh, that."

What had he thought? That plied with a little brandy she would be ready to jump his bones? Well, perhaps she was, but Louise still came first.

Exiting the bar into the night gave Isabel pause. "The temperature is still dropping." Her sweater was in the missing backpack. "And it smells like rain."

As she said it, a rumble in the distance punctuated the observation.

"Then we'd better be quick about it," Nick said, after which he remained strangely silent.

They raced up Milwaukee and then cut toward the raised railroad tracks. As they took the underpass to get to the north side, Isabel said, "I don't know about this." She didn't see any break, any way to get onto the railroad property. Either they were faced with a sheer drop or an incline protected by a chain-link fence. "I think we may be on a wild-goose chase."

And soon they would be chased by rain. The thunder rumbled closer, after which lightning split the night sky.

"Patience," Nick reminded her.

Rosalyn had been correct about the new construction, but Nick didn't let that—or her—stop him. He zigged around a half-completed house and zagged around the foundation of a second. And Isabel followed, all the while preparing herself for disappointment.

"Over there," he said, rushing forward toward a large tree that cut through the fencing.

Before she could comment that the supposed opening didn't look large enough, he stepped up on the knee of the tree where it stuck out from the hill, then squeezed himself between bark and steel, just as Rosalyn had told them she and Louise had done so many times. At his size, he barely made it through. Grabbing on to the fence post, Isabel took the step up and slid through more easily than she'd thought possible.

Nick's hands locked on to her waist and eased her descent. Her feet touched uneven ground, but he didn't let go immediately. They stood there, staring at each other, and Isabel was caught by the moment. Tension shivered through her and she didn't hurry to pull away. Thoughts about another night together sped up her pulse. She tried telling herself that her racing heartbeat was due to excitement at getting a step closer to her sister.

Then why did her knees seem to melt? And why
did she sway toward Nick until his head lowered and
his mouth loomed close enough to kiss.

Kiss!

Suddenly panicked, Isabel froze. She didn't want
to kiss Nick. Didn't want to fool herself. She knew
where she stood with him. Knew what he must think
of her for agreeing to his damn deal.

But when his lips touched hers, she couldn't pull
away. She didn't want to. She slipped her arms up
around his neck and gave in to her true desires, if
only for a moment.

Closing her eyes, she once again envisioned them
locked in a hot, naked embrace, just as if she were
watching a video of the act....

His front against her back, he wrapped one arm
securely around her waist and held her pinned onto
his length. And as she rocked, his free hand found
her breasts, coaxing her nipples into turgid peaks.

The erotic moment stretched into two and Nick's
hands slid down to lower, more dangerous territory.
Already beating too fast, her heart went into over-
drive, and before she lost her mind altogether, she
tried to salvage some of her common sense.

Tearing away from him, she gasped and said, "It
shouldn't be much farther."

Night was here and she knew what was coming.
Her body was more than ready, but they weren't
through searching for Louise. She had to get her mind
on something other than sex.

Her lips and other parts of her still tingling from
the encounter, she quickly headed toward the dark

blob a short distance away. As she walked, she pictured being reunited with her sister and clung to that image a if it were an anchor.

Thunder rolled and lightning forked the sky, illuminating the area ahead enough to see the dark blob turn into a small wooden structure with a flat corrugated metal roof. That had to be it!

Pulse pounding, Isabel quickened her step and unhooked the Maglite from her belt loop.

Be here, Lulu. Just please be here.

But when they drew closer and she called out, "Louise, are you inside?" no answering voice called back.

Isabel stopped in her tracks and faced the truth—another dead end.

"Aren't we going to check inside?" Nick asked.

She shrugged. "Since we're here, I suppose."

Raindrops splashing against her nose told her that if she didn't go inside, she would soon be soaked.

A step up took them to a door that opened with a rusty-hinged protest. Isabel flashed her light around. The small, low-ceilinged room with a single window on each side didn't look too bad. What appeared to be railroad ties were set out like a bench against the back wall, a city newspaper and crumpled bag before it.

"Fast food," Isabel murmured, able to smell the lingering odor.

Stooping, she checked the leavings that seemed fairly new and noted the logo on the paper bag. "From Louise's favorite fast-food place."

"Maybe we're closing in on her."

She picked up the newspaper and checked the date. "If she was here, it wasn't today. This paper is two days old." A patch of something white on the floor caught her eye. "What's that?" She picked up a scrap of paper. "A phone number." She flashed it at Nick, who took a good look but didn't comment. Then she stared at the plain block letters herself. "Louise *could* have written this. Thank heaven for cell phones." Hope renewed, she pulled hers from her pocket.

"You're going to call a number you found on the ground?"

"What can it hurt?"

Nick shrugged and sat back, but Isabel could feel his eyes on her as she punched in the number with a finger that trembled with excitement. Maybe this would be it, she thought, praying it would be. Two rings and there was an answer.

"Humboldt House" came the response, the voice female and light as if the speaker were young.

Her pulse trilled. "Uh, this is a shelter for teens, right?"

"Are you in trouble?"

"My sister, Louise," Isabel said breathlessly. "Lulu. Tall, pretty, long blond hair—"

"Who gave you this number?"

Isabel couldn't think quickly enough about what the right answer might be, so she tried the truth. "I, um, sort of found it. I think Louise dropped it and—"

"I'm sorry, you shouldn't be calling here."

A determined click brought the conversation—and her raised hopes—to an abrupt end.

"She hung up!" Isabel said incredulously, now convinced by the stir she'd caused that Humboldt House was indeed a runaway shelter.

"What did you expect?"

"Help, of course."

"A shelter *does* give help—to the victim."

"*I'm* not the reason she ran," Isabel said, hitting Redial.

"They don't know that."

Of course Nick made sense, she thought as the phone rang and rang. "Why doesn't someone answer?"

"Caller ID. I doubt they'll be taking your calls."

Frustration drove her to try again. She dialed a reverse directory and when the operator responded, said, "Yes. I need an address, probably in the Humboldt Park area. It's a shelter called Humboldt House." She read off the phone number.

Anxious for this new lead to pan out, Isabel fidgeted. A glance at Nick told her his gaze was focused on her, and her body warmed as if he were touching it.

"I'm sorry, ma'am," the operator said. "But that address is not available."

"What? Wait a minute!"

"Do you have another number?"

"No, but—"

"Then I'm sorry I couldn't help you today. Please try us again."

Closing her eyes in defeat, Isabel clicked off the phone and muttered, "The address is blocked."

"For the protection of the kids they're sheltering." Nick slid closer.

Trying not to be unnerved by his shoulder pressing against hers, she asked, "You know about Humboldt House?"

He hesitated only a moment before saying, "Yes."

"Why didn't you tell me about it?"

"What good would it have done if I couldn't provide you with the address?"

She nodded. "Maybe if we combed the neighborhood…"

"You think they advertise? Put a big sign outside?"

Isabel's insides felt twisted by the disappointment, and for the first time, she really wondered if she would ever find Louise. She couldn't think about her chances so negatively or it would drive her crazy.

Suddenly aware of a steady thrum beating at the corrugated-steel roofing, she said, "Uh-oh, it's raining really hard now."

"So we'll stay until it stops."

If it even did, Isabel thought, considering that the rain might keep up all night. "And then what?"

"We can go back to the abandoned building."

True. At least that one had running water. But so did they—it just happened to be outside. Unfortunately, the storm didn't sound as if it would be stopping anytime soon.

Great. They were stuck.

"If only I had a towel, I could get that shower out in the rain," she joked, longing for the amenities buried in her backpack and cursing the jerk who'd stolen it.

"Who needs a towel?" Nick asked. "It's summer. You can air dry."

"You mean waltz around naked? I'm not here for your entertainment."

"Funny, I thought you were."

Though he said it lightly, as if he were joking, heat shimmered through her as she remembered what Nick expected of her in exchange for his help.

She didn't say anything. She couldn't. Stuck at the back of her mind all day had been the knowledge that another night was racing closer with each hour that passed. She'd even pictured it so vividly she'd felt it. Trying to ignore it had given her temporary respite, but thoughts of her and Nick tangled together kept intruding more insistently, and now she was faced with the moment...

She shuddered with anticipation.

"Cold?" Nick asked, slipping an arm around her back and leaning in closer.

Lightning hit nearby, illuminating the shed. His features were taut and he was staring at her mouth.

"Maybe we should stretch out," he said, taking the Maglite from her and snapping it on. He ran the beam over the floor. "The good news is it's dry." He picked up the newspaper, opened the thick section and spread it sheet by sheet over a section of floor. "And now it's clean."

Taking the light from him, Isabel snapped it off and sat. She sensed more than saw Nick join her and lie back. They couldn't fully undress here. She knew that. But he would expect...well, she knew what he expected. Meeting those expectations would allow her not to think about other things for a while.

Before Isabel could so much as stretch out on her own, Nick had pulled her into his arms. Her head landed on his chest and she could hear the quick but steady beat of his heart. Her pulse was quickening, as well, and warmth spread through her as fast as a locomotive.

Railroad shed…locomotive… She snickered.

"Excuse me?" he whispered, his voice low and thick.

"Private joke."

"If you feel like letting me in, I'm eager," he said with a barely discernible smile.

She just bet he was. The play on words made her mind spin with uninvited images. And the more she thought about it…

"Is it hot in here," she murmured, "or is it just me?"

"You're hot, all right." This time they both laughed, and Nick slid down so they were face-to-face. "I always loved your laugh."

"You made me laugh more than anyone I've ever known. I've missed that," she admitted.

"What else have you missed?" he asked lightly.

Isabel's eyes fluttered closed. She'd missed everything about him. And when she felt his lips nudge hers, she thought maybe she'd missed that most of all—his kissing her. This kiss was slow and wet and she let herself drown in it. Time slipped away and she was a teenager again, experiencing the joy of love for the first time.

And when his hand captured her breast and held it gently, that, too, rushed her back to another time—safer, more innocent—when the future with its amazing possibilities was spread out before them. She wanted to lose herself in the past, even if just for a night.

When his lips left hers, she touched his face gently. Remembering the first time she'd almost lost her virginity, she scooted in the opposite direction, so that her legs lay along his head.

"What are you doing?" he whispered.

"What I know you'll like," she said, quickly unsnapping and unzipping his jeans.

"Isabel…"

"Do you want me to talk?" she asked, sliding a hand inside the opening. She found him through the briefs, then dipped her hand under that layer, too, until she found his heat. "Or do you want this?"

Nick groaned in answer as she clung to him with one hand while using the other to remove the impediments. Then he was exposed to her gaze, but not for long. Moistening her lips, she trailed them down his hardening length, then back up to the tip. She licked his head, sucked it, took it deeper.

"Isabel," Nick whispered, reaching for her.

Working her way back down his erection, she was aware of his hands on her. He was opening her jeans, slipping them down over her hips. The next thing she felt was warmth at her center through the material of her panties. She wondered if he remembered doing this before as clearly as she did—breathing through the panties so that she arched toward him…kissing her there, until she spread her thighs…invading her more deeply.

Riding her mouth, he sucked her through the thin material. Sensation flooded her and she imagined he was inside her. Realized he would be soon. His fingers hiked under the panties, where he stroked and probed, opening her to him.

Wishing he were truly inside her, she relaxed the back of her throat and took him deeper, trying to take all of him. He pushed her panties aside and tongued her so that she rocked her hips and teased his mouth.

Isabel hardly knew how he managed it, but Nick turned her so that she was spread more directly over him and he had more open access. He tugged her jeans down to her knees. And then her panties. The moment his finger slid inside her, she was ready to come.

The touch of his tongue against her clit drove her to new heights and she relaxed the back of her throat and finally took him all in. He did the same, covering her completely with his mouth. Isabel gasped and came up for air but immediately took him in again. She wanted him, wanted him now. She rocked against his mouth while he arched into hers.

Within seconds, she felt the pulsing begin. His. Hers. She closed her eyes and lost herself in the pleasure of the hot come shooting down her throat, and in her own orgasm that seemed to go on forever.

And when it ended and Isabel collapsed on her side, Nick pulled her up toward him. Still tasting him, she closed her eyes and admitted to herself that she wanted more.

More sex.

Just more.

That was the danger, the thing she'd been secretly dreading. What if there wasn't more? What if this was all she would ever have of him?

So what did that make her? she wondered. What kind of woman traded sex for favors when she wanted something more?

And that something was the one thing she would never ask for. Probably never get. Certainly not from Nick. Maybe not from anyone but her little sister.

There were various words she could use to describe that missing something, but the one that kept coming back to her was the most dangerous, the scariest of them all…

Love.

10

"THE RAIN FINALLY STOPPED," Nick told Isabel the moment she opened her eyes the next morning. He'd been awake for hours watching her, and with his thoughts all stirred up, his mood had turned sour and he was impatient to move on. "We can get out of here anytime. Just say the word."

"Good morning to you, too," she croaked. "Get up on the wrong side of the bed this morning?"

"Something like that."

Rather, the wrong side of Isabel.

The sex had been hard and fast, and though he'd come, it hadn't been satisfying in the way he wanted it to be.

In the middle of the night while she'd slept the sleep of the exhausted, he'd spooned her, he'd touched her soft places, smelled her hair, longed for her to...well, longed for something he doubted he would ever have with her.

And the guilt at what he'd coerced her to do—whether or not he'd meant to do it—was eating at him. He'd spent the last hour agonizing over it.

Isabel yawned and stretched. Her hair was a bird's nest, her clothes disheveled, her face puffy with sleep.

And yet he thought her the most beautiful mess he'd ever seen.

"Isabel, I think we should call this quits. I'll see you home and—"

"No! You can't!"

"Don't worry, I'll find Louise for you," he said.

Her forehead furrowed. "What?"

"I'll do it. I promise."

Isabel's visage lightened, and certain that she would be relieved, Nick was surprised when she shook her head.

"I appreciate the offer," she said, "but we're going to find her together."

"What? You don't trust me?"

"I want to finish what we started." She licked her lips as she always did when she was nervous. "I, uh, was thinking that maybe my seeing this through to the finish would give me what I need. Um, I was hoping I could actually do something positive with what I've learned." Quickly, she added, "And don't you dare laugh."

"I wouldn't think of it," he said, wondering what she was getting at.

"Being out on the streets just for a short while has been eye-opening—and gut-wrenching, too. If I could make other people feel that way, I mean, let them see what it's like through my eyes…"

"You mean write about this."

She nodded. "Stupid?"

He stared at her as if he'd never seen her before. Then he smiled. "That's great. Really great."

And then another great thing happened. They were

smiling at each other, and in that second, the unexpected connection wiped out the gloom of the morning.

"Then it's settled," Isabel said. "I stick with you until we find Louise. Together." She poked at her bird's nest and groused, "Of all the things I had in my backpack, the things I miss most are my comb and my toothbrush."

"We'll stop at a drugstore so you can replace them."

"Good. What about you?"

"I have a toothbrush in my pocket. The fold-up kind like you take on camping trips." Not that he'd ever been on an actual camping trip. His "campouts" had never been of the traditional variety. "If you can't wait, I'd be happy to lend it to you."

"I can hang on a little while longer. I never imagined it would seem like a luxury to brush my teeth. Or *shower*," she said pointedly.

"All right." He checked his watch to make sure they had time to make it. "If you really want a shower, then a shower you shall have."

"Thank you," she murmured, shoving her billed cap back over the bird's nest and leading the way out the door.

"ANOTHER PARK?" ISABEL ASKED, stopping dead in her tracks. Although they'd picked up a comb and toothbrush, she hadn't had a morning cup of coffee and the lack of caffeine was making her irritable. "I thought we were going to get showers first thing."

"We are." Nick kept on, heading straight for the field house.

"I don't understand," she said, chasing after him.

"The bigger park districts have pools and showers for anyone who needs them. It's how people without other options can stay clean."

People like her sister was what he meant. She could see that he wanted to increase her learning curve, and now that she had something positive to do with the knowledge, she was all for it. Not that she wasn't nervous about the prospect. These new experiences were definitely unsettling, and she was finding that her usual confidence was difficult to conjure.

Another thing she should take note of for the story—how taking away a safety net could change the person you thought you were….

"Are you sure they'll let us in?" she asked.

"Positive. Showers are open to the public before nine in the morning and after nine at night."

Even so, Isabel felt weird entering the field house, especially when the guy at the desk asked, "Can I help you?"

"Which way to the showers?" Nick asked.

An expression of surprise and something else crossed the worker's face, but he quickly covered it and pointed down the hall. "You have about twenty minutes to be in and out of there," he warned.

Isabel felt her neck grow hot as if the guy's eyes were burning into her while she hurried inside the women's locker room. A few of the women were swimmers who were either readying themselves to get in the pool or had already done their laps. But if the grimy backpack on the shower-stall hook and black plastic bags she spotted on the floor were any indication, the other women were there for the showers alone.

Isabel picked a locker and found clothes inside. So she wasn't the only one without a lock. The next one she checked was empty. She sat to remove her shoes and surreptitiously examined the other women who weren't there to use the pool.

The owner of the backpack stepped out of her shower. She appeared to be a teenager like Louise. Another shabbily dressed woman with a toddler in tow heading for the exit was probably in her mid-twenties. And then she spotted two women just short of elderly.

Not wanting to think about them too closely, Isabel looked away. Wondering if her father was at the office yet, she decided to give calling him a try.

He picked up on the third ring. "Grayson here."

"It's Isabel," she said in a low tone, giving her back to the other women in the area so they couldn't hear. "We just missed her yesterday at the club, but we have another chance to catch up with her tonight."

"Where?"

"A rave in an old warehouse west of the Loop." Phone pressed between ear and shoulder, she untied a shoe. "It's that vacant one off of Lake Street."

"What *is* Louise thinking—"

"And I have another lead I want to follow," Isabel interrupted before he blew up. She got the other shoe off and threw both into the locker. "Only I can't get the information I need. Maybe you can."

"What kind of information?" he growled.

"An address for a place called Humboldt House. I'm pretty sure it's a privately funded runaway shelter for kids, but I haven't been able to obtain the address myself."

"I'll get someone on it right away," he promised.

"Good." A sudden scuffle from the other side of the locker room startled her and set her heart racing. *What now?* "I have to go. I'll call back later."

BY THE TIME HE HEARD the click on the other end, he had her location. She was barely a mile away…he could get to her in minutes.

Smart move on his part that he'd made sure she had one of the new cell phones with GPS technology built in before he'd even known it would come in so handy. He congratulated himself on a job well-done.

Scientists who'd developed the Global Positioning Satellite surely hadn't thought their work would be so deadly….

ISABEL HAD BARELY PUT the cell phone back in her pocket when a young voice cried out, "I didn't steal your stuff. Let me go!"

She whipped around the row of lockers in time to see the teenager, now dressed, shove one of the older women, grab her backpack and run out.

"I'll report you and you won't be taking any more showers in here!" the woman called after her.

"Like I would want your garbage," the girl muttered, flying by Isabel and almost knocking into her.

And before she disappeared around the corner, Isabel noted the girl's expression—guilt warring with desperation. A sick feeling shot through her.

That could be Louise.

"What am I going to do now?" the older woman cried.

Her friend said, "You'll find new stuff, Martha."

"But I had enough money for food for a few days."

"We can make signs, stand out on a busy street corner."

As she went back to her locker and took off her shoes and socks, Isabel thought she couldn't stand it. Which was worse—a teenager stealing to survive or an old woman having to beg for enough money for food? About to undress, she couldn't shut out the woman's sobs. Something inside her gave. She raided her wallet for her reserves. After all, *she* had alternatives.

When she rounded the lockers again, the friend was still comforting the victim, who sat on a bench. A couple of other women in swimsuits ignored them as if they didn't exist and headed toward the pool door. Shaking her head, Isabel stepped forward, money folded in her hand so as not to be obtrusive.

"Excuse me?"

The victim looked up at her through red-rimmed eyes. "I didn't mean to disturb no one." Her voice quivered and she swallowed hard.

"No, it's all right," Isabel said, crouching before her. "I want you to have this." She took the hand that had seen stronger days, pressed the bills into the palm and curled the frail fingers around it. "Get food and shelter for the night."

"Bless you, child!" the woman said as Isabel backed off. "You're an honest-to-goodness saint."

Isabel hurried back to her locker, where she started to undress. Aware that she had no towel to cover herself, she grew self-conscious when one of the swimmers glowered at her and moved over, as if she were afraid that Isabel might contaminate her.

Worrying about leaving her own wallet with her identification in an open locker, Isabel emptied the plastic bag of her toothbrush, paste, comb and travel-size vial of hair spray she'd convinced Nick to let her buy. She dropped the wallet in, then brought the bag into the shower with her.

How weird that after so short a time on the street she was already thinking in ways different than normal. Something she would have to include in her story, she thought.

The water was barely warm, the stream barely adequate, but the shower pouring over her felt like heaven. She pumped out antiseptic-smelling liquid soap from the wall dispenser and lathered not only her body but her hair.

She could have stayed under the water all day, but Nick would be waiting for her, so, reluctantly, she shut down the shower and used her hands to slick the excess water from her body. Then she took advantage of the hand dryers set high so swimmers could dry their hair. Though the signs warned patrons not to dry their clothing with them, Isabel defiantly washed out her panties and did so, anyway.

For several minutes, the whine was the only sound she heard. When it stopped and she pulled on her clean panties, the locker room was eerily quiet. She looked around, blinking in surprise.

At last, she was alone.

NO ONE EVEN LOOKED UP as he strolled down the field house hallway, hands in pockets, head down in a non-threatening manner, billed cap pulled down to his sunglasses, the two together half hiding his face.

At first, not seeing her outside, he'd thought he'd arrived at the park too late. Then Novak had exited the field house looking fresh as a daisy, his hair still damp. That had tipped him off as to where to find her. Novak hadn't even noticed him when they'd passed each other.

Opening a janitor's closet, he pulled free a stanchion with a Closed for Cleaning warning. He checked the hallway once more. All clear. Then he headed for the women's locker room, intending on using the sign to keep new arrivals out. First he stopped at the water fountain and washed down a little something that would keep him on track.

He opened the door and carefully peered inside, hoping against hope that she would be alone. At first he saw no one. Then he moved inside, back against the tile wall, and spotted her. She was dressed and trying to get a comb through her tangled hair.

His pulse thudded and his skin flushed with a combination of anticipation and dread.

After all, he'd never before actually taken a human life.

ISABEL HAD JUST FINISHED combing and tying back her hair. She was about to give it a spray so that it would stay out of her face when the lights went out.

"What the…?" she muttered. Then, louder, she called out, "Hey, anyone else in here?"

Even though she knew the place was deserted, that someone must have overloaded the ancient circuit somewhere else in the building, she couldn't stop her pulse from jagging as she felt for the tiled wall. She would follow it to the entrance. Opening the door would let in enough light so that she could retrieve her few things left in the locker.

She slid around a corner and directly into something solid. Hand out, she felt warm flesh.

"Ah!" she yelped, jumping back.

But the warm flesh followed, a hard hand grabbing onto her arm, twirling her around in a circle and smashing her into the wall so the very breath was knocked out of her.

Gasping, she said, "Hey, who the hell do you th—"

Her words were cut off by the feel of a vise against her throat. Strong hands. Male.

Panic made Isabel rip at them, but they wouldn't budge. She futilely fought for air. Starting to feel faint, she struck out, raking soft flesh with her nails.

"Bitch!" came the low male growl that echoed through the dark, empty locker room.

His grip loosened a fraction and she used leverage to dance him around. Then, his weight pressing on hers once more, he jammed her back into the lockers and her head hit the edge of the door she'd left open. Stunned, she couldn't move.

The fingers squeezed tighter and lights telegraphed inside her head, signaling her own death if she didn't do something fast. He was stronger than she—fighting seemed useless.

She needed a weapon.

She threw out her hand and found air. The open locker. Remembering the few items Nick had let her buy, she awkwardly scrambled for them.

The one she wanted was just out of reach....

"Die, bitch!" her attacker whispered.

Coaxing the item forward with the tips of her fingers, she finally got hold of it. And with the last reserve of her strength, praying her aim was true, she pressed down on the trigger.

"Aaaah!"

The attacker's hands freed her throat, no doubt to go to his eyes. Hair spray had never seemed so important before!

Finding strength she didn't know she had, Isabel shoved him and kept shoving until he backed into the bench. She couldn't see but imagined the wood slab had caught him calf height and toppled him backward. An explosion of metal told her he'd hit the lockers.

Then Isabel made even more noise, screaming as she felt her way to the hall door.

"Help! Nick!" She flew into the hall so fast, she had to catch herself on the opposite wall. "Nick!"

"What the hell's going on there?" This from the

green-shirted guy at the desk. "You high on something?"

Rushing toward him, she forced out the words. "I was attacked!"

"Listen, you street people can use the facilities, but I'm not getting in the middle of any argument."

"No, a man!" she said, her throat straining to get the words out even as Nick came flying back through the door. "A man attacked me!"

"What happened?" Nick demanded.

"Locker room," she gasped, hand to her throat. "He tried to strangle me."

Nick flew down the hall, Isabel following, the park district guy yelling, "Hey, he can't go in there!"

"Watch me!" Nick yelled without turning from his purpose.

Isabel was right behind him when he ripped open the locker room door. The lights were on and they rushed inside. A nude woman quickly pulled her towel around herself and screamed bloody murder.

Isabel looked around wildly, but there was no sign of a man. The only indication that the attack had happened at all was the canister of hair spray on the floor.

"I swear I left him right there," she said, pointing to the now empty bench.

The lone woman had backed behind the lockers but was still screaming.

The employee was on them, and he had brought muscle with him. The second guy looked like he could bench-press his own considerable weight. The two men grabbed Nick and dragged him toward the locker room door.

"The lady was attacked!" Nick yelled. "You're letting the bastard get away!"

"The only ones who are going to get away are you two," the first employee said as the duo pulled a struggling Nick toward the field house door. They shoved him outside and Isabel with him. "And don't either of you come back or I'll call the cops!"

"ARE YOU ALL RIGHT?" Nick asked, helping Isabel to a bench in the shade.

Sitting, Isabel nodded. She didn't look all right. She looked stunned and scared. He slid next to her on the bench and pulled her to him, cradling her gently for a moment. Her heart seemed to thunder against his and her flesh seemed to melt under his hands.

For a moment, she was his. He pressed his cheek against her hair and ran a hand along her spine. When she sighed and reached trembling arms up to circle his neck, something inside him melted, as well.

If anything had happened to her...

Nick found her mouth and kissed her softly, reassuringly. She kissed him back hard, as if the connection would console her. When he stroked her hair and her neck, Isabel sighed and loosened her grip on him and sat back. She looked so beautiful. Face freshly scrubbed, hair shiny again, she was as lovely as any angel.

"What happened in there?" he asked.

"The place went dark and when I tried to find my way out, some guy grabbed me and threw me back against the wall. H-he tried to choke me."

Her hand strayed to her neck. Frowning, Nick saw the beginnings of bruises. He cursed and said, "Maybe we'd better call the cops ourselves."

"No! No cops. The park district people think we're the troublemakers. *We* would probably be the ones to end up in jail." She shook her head. "I don't understand how he got away."

"Probably through the pool area."

Nick would argue with her about calling the police, but he didn't think it would do much good. Besides, they had just entered a treaty of sorts, and he didn't want to do anything to upset her.

His mind was whirling. Could this possibly be a coincidence? First someone following them, then Isabel being pushed into the street and now being attacked?

He wondered if she'd put it together herself. If she'd drawn the same conclusion as he.

He didn't want to put his speculation into words. Didn't want to ask her about her father's secrets again. She was upset enough. He didn't need to scare her to death.

But how could he not try to protect her?

"Did you get a look at the guy?"

"I told you, the lights went out. I couldn't even identify him."

"I wonder. I don't think that was just some guy looking for easy pickings. I think he was after you."

"Why?"

"You tell me."

Her expression hardened, but she remained tight-lipped on the subject.

"All right, then, don't tell me," Nick said, tired of her misplaced loyalty. "But I think it's time to leave this whole thing to the authorities."

"No!"

"It's become too dangerous."

"If *I'm* in danger, then think about Louise. I won't abandon her! But you don't have to do this. Go if you want."

"I'm not the victim here," Nick reminded her. "I wasn't suggesting I would abandon you. But what if we *can't* find your sister?" he asked, shifting at his own duplicity.

He now had a good idea of where they *might* find Louise, though he couldn't share that information with Isabel lest he betray the code. Kids on the street trusted him because he kept their secrets.

"Don't say that. We almost found her last night."

"You're playing with your sister's life here. And your own."

Seeming dazed, she shook her head. "I just don't understand why!"

He could see she didn't. Whatever she'd been holding back about the senator didn't seem like a big enough deal to her to have anyone come after them.

Maybe she *didn't* know everything, Nick speculated. But maybe whoever had pushed her in front of the car and attacked her inside the locker room thought she did.

"I'll make you a deal," he said. "I'll keep looking with you. We'll go to that rave tonight. But if we don't find Louise by then, we go to the authorities."

He could see she was weakening. Fear for one's

life did that to a person. And she also had Louise's safety to think about.

"If we don't find her by tonight...then I'll think about it," she agreed.

It was all he was going to get from her. Such incredible loyalty...he only hoped she got what she needed from her father in return.

In the meantime, he needed to protect her.

"Ready to make some more rounds?" he asked, figuring doing something positive would take her mind off what had happened to her for the moment. "There's a drop-in center that provides food and referrals for teens on the street—"

"That sounds promising."

"It's in a rough neighborhood a couple of miles from here," he warned her.

"I don't care what kind of neighborhood. I care about finding my sister."

"We may not find her at this place," he said, knowing he was probably wasting their time. He wondered if he shouldn't look into Humboldt House. But even if Louise took refuge at the shelter at night, she would probably be on the move during the day. So it was likely futile to check it out now. "As I said, it's some distance from here." A good thing since he wanted to get Isabel as far away from this area as possible, to give her a chance to feel safe. "It's a real long shot."

"One I'm willing to take."

Good. He stood and held out his hand to her. "Let's get over to the bus stop, then."

Isabel raised her eyebrows and rose without his

help. "Great, you're finally willing to take public transportation when I just gave away all my money to a couple of homeless women."

Happy that Isabel Grayson had a heart after all, Nick grinned at her. "Then it'll be my treat."

One he owed her, anyway, for leading her down the garden path, so to speak. But it was a path that would give her more information for the piece she'd decided to write.

Equally important, Nick acknowledged, they would be together.

How had this happened? He hadn't wanted to see her again and now he didn't want to let her go.

What he wanted was to make love to her as if nothing bad had ever happened between them. He wanted her to kiss him with passion and emotion and to love him again.

No, not *again*, he reminded himself. She'd never loved him in the first place. She'd merely experimented with him. She'd said so.

The thought tempered his good mood, and as Nick led Isabel to the bus stop, he kept an eye out around them for anything—or anyone—that looked out of place.

He might not have her for long, but he had her for now, and he was going to keep her safe.

11

TWENTY MINUTES LATER they entered Haven, a double storefront where two adults were busy dealing with a number of teens of various socioeconomic backgrounds. Closer at hand was a bulletin board with announcements about the services Haven offered—Isabel scanned notices about group counseling, drug programs, job-finding assistance.

Nothing about danger. About potential murderers on the streets.

While she'd put on a good face for the moment—something she was expert at—Isabel was more frightened than she'd ever been in her life.

A smell wafted to her that made her stomach growl in response. "Coffee." A big pot was set out on a nearby table. "Do you think anyone would mind?"

"Knock yourself out," Nick said.

As she filled a paper cup, she went over everything in her head once more. No, someone trying to choke her to death still didn't make sense. Infidelity didn't add up to murder. No matter that Nick had raised the question in her mind, she wanted to believe that attack was a coincidence.

Odd, though, that it had come on the heels of her being pushed into the street the night before....

When the cup was full, she couldn't wait. As she poured for Nick, she took a long, satisfying swig and imagined the caffeine went straight to her brain. Unfortunately, it didn't leave her any less confused.

Her father might not show his love for her, but she was certain he didn't want her dead, no matter what she knew about him. Her father was many things, not all of them good, but he was no murderer.

Taking another swig, she murmured appreciatively and handed Nick a cup.

When he tasted it, he grimaced. "You like this stuff?"

"Beggars can't be choosers," she murmured, eyeing the box of doughnuts, as well.

"Have one," came a male voice from behind them.

Isabel turned as a short middle-aged man wearing a T-shirt, jeans and long curly hair stepped up to greet them.

"Jerry Kramer," he said. "What can I do for you folks?"

Isabel took Kramer up on his doughnut offer and Nick introduced them and told him about Louise.

"Do you have a photo?"

"I did, but my backpack was stolen." She swallowed and realized her throat was sore, probably bruised inside as well as out. "She kind of looks like me—Louise is my younger sister."

The social worker was already shaking his head. "Can't say I've seen her around here."

"What about a runaway shelter?" Isabel's pulse thrummed as she asked, "Humboldt House—do you have the address?"

Kramer's friendly expression closed a bit. "Sorry, I can't give you that information."

"Because you don't have it or because you don't want to?"

"Because I can't," Kramer repeated. "What I can do is offer you the message board. If your sister comes in, she'll see it. If she wants to contact you, she will."

Losing it, Isabel said, "She already has that option!"

Nick put his hand on her arm. "Calm down."

"Right! My sister is on the streets, someone is after me, maybe both of us, and I'm not supposed to be upset?"

"After you?" the social worker repeated. "If you're in trouble—"

"My sister's the one in trouble."

Before he probed too deeply, Isabel agreed to leave the message. Once done, they left Haven and Nick suggested they get something to eat.

"No money," she reminded him, then added with hope, "The ATM?"

"A more time-honored way." With a flourish, he held out his hand.

"You mean panhandling?"

Tension wired through Isabel as she thought about begging for money. But it was part of the experience, she told herself. If she wanted her view of life on the street to be accurate, panhandling was part of it. The streets were tough. If she hadn't fully understood that before, she certainly did now. And she wasn't about to back out of the agreement.

"Ironic, isn't it?" she muttered. "I give away my money so that a woman I don't even know won't have to do what I'm now going to do to eat." She glanced at Nick. "Don't worry, I'm not changing my mind. We'll do it your way."

"I should be able to do it my way sometime, don't you think?" he asked with a grin.

They weren't talking about dinner money anymore.

From Nick's expression, he was thinking of whatever it was they would be doing later. Of how he would like to take her.

So far she'd been pretty much in control of their close encounters. The message that he might want to take the lead sent the blood thrumming through her veins and her imagination soaring.

How would he approach her?

Him on top? Beneath? Behind?

She could picture them together each and every way. The video ran again in her head and it was definitely X-rated. Now it showed an image of him on top, inside her, arms hooked under her knees, lifting them until she curled her feet around the back of his neck. Not that she even knew whether or not she was limber enough...

Isabel tried to swallow, but her throat still hurt and her mouth was suddenly too dry and her thoughts were suddenly too jumbled. Thinking about being with Nick again inflamed her and yet she didn't want *just* to have sex with him....

Knowing longing for more was useless, she asked, "So where do I get my tin cup?"

"I'm afraid paper will have to do."

Once they arrived at their location, he reached into a street container and fetched a paper cup that had originated in a designer coffee shop. When he wiped it off, it looked clean enough. Still, Isabel wished she'd thought of sticking a pair of latex gloves in her pocket.

Six-corner intersections were a favored spot for indigents to panhandle—not only lots of cars, but lots of foot traffic. However, this one was too close to home for her comfort. What if someone she knew passed by? Isabel pulled the billed cap low over her forehead and prayed that no one would recognize her.

She stood at the curb alone so she could solicit both pedestrians on the sidewalk and cars on the street. Rather than sticking to her side, Nick retreated and stood with his back against a building so that it wouldn't look like they were together. His reasoning was that a woman would make more money if she was alone and appeared desperate.

She was desperate, all right.

Wearing clothes that needed to be washed and having hair that needed to be combed made her look indigent, she guessed. But her sense of panic at having to beg enough money for a meal is what made her *feel* desperate. She couldn't even look at herself in a nearby store window.

But she sure could write about how humiliating this felt, she thought as a man approached. "Spare change?"

"I only have bills," he said, then continued walking without giving her one.

This was an experience she would never forget.

To several people crossing the street, she asked, "Could you spare a quarter?"

One woman said, "Go get a job!"

Another gave her a contemptuous look. "You'll only spend it on liquor or drugs. I won't support your addiction."

Isabel wanted to crawl into a hole somewhere.

Over the next half hour, some coins dropped in the cup. A few bills. But most of the drivers looked the other way and pedestrians didn't say anything, merely walked past her without actually looking at her, all making her feel as if she really weren't there.

It was a surreal sensation and yet one that was all too familiar. Isn't that the way her father treated her more often than not?

Her putting herself out here to be insulted and humiliated was *his* fault, Isabel thought. Why had she agreed to clean up this mess for him? A bad habit, she admitted, knowing it was one she had to break. In the past, her father had always had good, solid political reasons for what he'd asked her to do. But not this time.

And this time, she thought, again thinking about illuminating the public about life on the street, she would look to a different future.

A car pulled up to the curb and a window rolled down and Isabel snapped to.

"Spare change?" she asked the driver. "It's for food, honest."

He immediately pulled out a twenty and waved it at her. "C'mon. Get in. I've got a half hour. We can drive over to the park and—"

"I'm not going anywhere with you. Get lost!"

The driver opened the door and got out of his car. "What, I'm not good enough for you?"

"The lady told you to get lost."

Suddenly Nick was there next to her, placing a protective arm around her shoulders and challenging the man with his very presence. Shaking inside, Isabel leaned into him, grateful for his presence. But how many young girls had someone to protect *them?*

The guy got back into his car and ripped through the changing lights, setting off several sets of blaring horns.

"He thought I was going to..." Isabel shook off her anger. "That's it, I'm through here." She looked into the cup with its several dollars' worth of change. "Hmm, think this is enough to get a meal?"

"Let's check it out."

Isabel followed Nick to a nearby restaurant that was no more than a hole in the wall, a place she would never think of entering. But the service was fast and friendly and the meat loaf and mashed potatoes were better and cheaper than she'd expected. Nick didn't try to start a conversation with her until her appetite was sated.

"Feeling better?" he asked.

"My stomach is."

"But you're not?"

"What do you think?" she asked. "Out there, I felt like something someone scraped off the bottom of their shoe."

"That kind of feeling is enough to wreck anyone's self-confidence. And the number of kids on the street is growing and will keep growing until the right pro-grams are put in place.''

''If you wanted my help through official channels, why didn't you simply ask in the first place?''

''Because I didn't think you would listen with an open mind. The problem never touched you until now. I wanted you to get the big picture.''

She nodded. ''I guess I see your point. I just hope I can now help others get the message.''

Though if she left her father's employ, she would cut herself off from a channel for change. She might write about it, but what then? She was damned if she did and damned if she didn't.

But in the meantime…had she been wrong about Nick's motives from the beginning? She'd seen his taking her to the streets as an act of pure revenge. But now she wasn't so certain. His shooting footage for the documentary on the plight of runaway kids must have opened his eyes fast. And his heart. When they'd started out on their journey, she hadn't been certain he'd had one.

For his caring and sense of purpose alone, she could forgive him anything in the present.

The question was…would he ever find it in that heart of his to forgive her for the past?

THOUGH HE HADN'T ADMITTED as much to Isabel, Nick had thought her heartless when she'd shown up at his door, even though she had been looking for her sister. Considering the cruel way in which she'd blown him off, how else should he have felt?

Now, after having spent so much time with her, he

knew differently. But if Isabel *wasn't* heartless, what the hell had happened all those years before? He studied her as if he could get some answers. But all he saw was a discouraged woman close to exhaustion.

"You look tired," he said.

"Maybe because I am."

He checked his watch. "We have hours to kill before the rave."

"What? You don't have some learning activity planned for me until then?"

But she wasn't too tired to be sarcastic, he noted. "I'm fresh out."

"Then what shall we do? Go sit on a park bench?"

"How about getting some rest?"

"We're close to the town house." She let out a laugh. "Wouldn't that frost my father if he found us together in his own home?"

"I have someplace more basic in mind."

"I'll just bet you do." Isabel sighed. "Well, let's go, then."

Undoubtedly Isabel would think he was trying to torture her further, but all he wanted was to make certain that she was safe. She might not believe it, but Nick was certain her attacker knew her. Or was working for someone who did.

Her father? He shuddered at the thought.

Whoever he was, the bastard knew about him, as well. Probably even knew where he lived. So Nick wasn't about to chance delivering Isabel into a would-be murderer's hands. His hope was that they would find Louise that night and all would become clear.

And then he would convince Isabel to go to the authorities regardless of the consequences.

In the meantime, he would protect her. But from whom?

Nick had no respect for Senator William Grayson, but found it hard to believe the man could actually want his own daughter dead. She'd always gone out of her way to please her father, to do exactly as he'd wanted, as if she feared he wouldn't love her otherwise. Had that included dumping her socially unacceptable boyfriend? For years he'd believed she'd never loved him, but now he wondered if there hadn't been something else going on that he hadn't understood.

This Isabel wasn't the woman he'd imagined she would have become. She seemed to care about people, maybe even about him. At the thought, his unease about their deal grew by leaps and bounds.

He'd used the proposition as a weapon against her, to drive her away, but the plan had backfired. Then she'd turned it back on him. Now he was hooked—big time—and feeling too guilty for words.

No more, he thought. No matter how much he wanted her, no more.

For the most important thing he'd learned in the past few days was how much he still loved Isabel Grayson.

12

By THE TIME NICK SHUTTLED Isabel off the second bus, her jangled nerves had caught up with her and squirrels seemed to be performing back flips in her stomach. Where the heck was he taking her?

Being west of the Loop, she could see the city high-rises and figured they couldn't be too far from the warehouse where the rave was to be held.

"This way," Nick said, leading her down a deserted street whose buildings were mostly shuttered.

"Where are you taking me?"

"Somewhere safe."

Safe. A relative word. She'd felt safe until that morning, until she'd almost been choked to death. She and her sister were both in danger, though she still couldn't say why. Knowing she might never feel safe again, she wondered if Louise would be able to give her the reason. Could Louise have the key? Did her sister know something more than she? Something that could get them both killed?

"That's it," Nick said, pointing straight ahead.

All she saw was an old viaduct that ran under a raised street. The opening was blocked with chain-link fencing.

"Come on." He walked right up to the barrier. "Let's get in there fast, before anyone spots us."

He did mean the viaduct! He scaled the chain link as if he were expert at it.

"Nick, are you crazy?"

He was already at the top of the fence. Swinging a leg over, he balanced and held out his hand to her. Knowing better than to argue with him, she followed, thankful for the gym time that kept her in good shape. A slim opening at the top allowed him to drop down on the other side. Then, as she carefully descended, he placed his hands around her waist, easing her to solid ground.

Heart thudding at his touch, she turned in his arms and felt her breath sweep away at the thought he might kiss her. For the first time since they'd come together, she actually wanted him to—without reservations.

Though they were cast in shadow, she got a brief glimpse of his expression…and then he turned away. Something she'd seen in his eyes called to her deepest being.

"How do you know this place?" she asked.

"It's been here forever."

"But it's kind of out of the way," she said, raising her voice to be heard over the traffic noise above them. "Why would you have come here?"

"Because it was safe." He turned from her and went deeper into the shadows. "No predators."

"Predators? Like wolves."

"Like people who prey on kids."

"Runaways?"

He didn't answer, but from the way his back stiffened, she knew. She finally understood. How had she been so blind that she hadn't realized it before this?

Nick had been on the streets himself.

That was why he was so savvy about where to look. That was why he had the connection with the kids. That was why he was shooting the documentary.

"When?" she asked softly.

"Off and on through high school. Before that. It was the reason I fell behind in school."

She remembered him going missing only to reappear days, even weeks, later. And then he had just disappeared…until she'd found him a few days ago.

"Why, Nick? What happened?"

He turned toward her, but she couldn't see his face. He was a dark silhouette against the light at the other side of the tunnel.

"My mother was one of those women who couldn't or wouldn't take care of herself," Nick said. "She always needed a man to do that. And after my dad left…let's say I had several 'uncles,' not one of them the kind of man who appreciated someone else's by-blow."

She winced at his bluntness. "Didn't your mother care how they treated you? Or how you felt?"

"My mother's main concern was that someone else foot the responsibility for her life. She sold herself for what she thought was security."

The harsh words cut her to the quick. She couldn't even imagine the kind of life he'd been forced into. He must have been so unhappy…except when they'd been together. Isabel was certain that he'd been happy with her.

And she'd taken that from him.

Isabel went to Nick and put her arms around him. "I'm sorry," she whispered. "I'm so, so sorry."

"Why? What did you do this time?"

"I drove you away. But I had to, Nick. I had no choice."

"We all have choices."

"I didn't want you to go to jail," she told him, and figured that was probably the last thing he expected to hear. He stiffened.

"What?"

"My father found out that we slept together," she admitted. "He told me that either I would stop seeing you...or that he would have you arrested for aggravated sexual assault."

"I didn't force you to do anything you didn't want to do. Did I?"

"No, of course not, but you were eighteen, a legal adult, and I was only sixteen. Aggravated sexual assault, Nick. My father would have said that you coerced me and would have seen that you were punished."

"My life was ruined, anyway," he said. "My latest 'uncle' liked to slap people around. One day I stepped between him and my mother and he used me as a punching bag, after which my mother told me to get out. She said I was old enough to be on my own, that she couldn't provide for me anymore, that she needed to take care of herself. And I went looking for you to tell you what happened and that I would call you as soon as I found a place to stay.''

The true horror of that night so long ago chilled Isabel. ''Oh, no, and I said all those awful things to you.''

''Better to have sat in some jail cell than to have gone through the hell of believing you never cared. Isabel, why didn't you just tell me the truth?''

''Would you have agreed to a breakup?''

He shook his head. ''I loved you more than my life.''

''That's what I was afraid of, because that's how I felt about you. I couldn't let you go to jail, Nick, so I did what I had to. I drove you away the only way I knew how.''

He laughed. ''How ironic. I would have gone, anyway, because my mother gave me no choice. And even if I *had* landed in jail, at least I would have had hope in my heart. Something…someone…*you*…to come back to.''

''Nick, please understand—''

''Understand what?'' he demanded. ''That you convinced yourself that you had to do it? Be honest, Isabel. For once in your life, be really honest. Your father never would have made a federal case of it. He wouldn't have wanted to look bad in the eyes of his constituents. And his political ambitions went way beyond where he was then. He wouldn't have compromised them. He bluffed and you folded. Part of you wanted your father's approval and love so badly that you would have done anything he wanted you to do, including dumping me.''

Swallowing hard, she whispered, "That's not true!"

"Isn't it?" Nick moved away and changed his tone. "There's grass over here and it's soft and reasonably clean." He sat on the incline and patted the area next to him. "Come on over. You ought to lie down and try to get some sleep."

It was as if he had rid himself of all emotion. He was almost as good at pretending as she, Isabel thought.

"I don't do naps," she told him.

Could he be right? Had she used her father's threat as an excuse?

"Make this an exception."

"I'll just wake up cranky and try to make you as miserable as I feel."

"And that would be different...how?" he said wryly.

Certain that he was putting on a good face to diffuse the tension between them, Isabel couldn't so much as raise a smile. There was too much to be sad about. The things he'd told her about his past. His belief that she'd dumped him to please her father. The short amount of time they had left together.

Either they would find Louise tonight or she would bring in the authorities. Nick was right about that. Either way, this would undoubtedly be the last time she and Nick would be together alone.

Isabel felt as if a great hole were spreading through her middle. The gap inside her that had started to close by being with Nick was widening once more.

She stared down at him, lying on his back. This

couldn't be all there was. She still loved him…had always loved him. How was she going to go on without him again?

Stretching out next to him, Isabel ran her hand down his flat stomach and over his jean flap. His instant response spread through her, and she coaxed him to erection until he caught her wrist and stopped her.

"Don't," he whispered.

She drew closer to him. Her body was coming alive in anticipation of his. This was their last chance to be together and she wasn't going to pass it up.

"What, then?" she whispered, bringing his hand to her breast.

For a brief moment, his fingers curled around her soft flesh. His thumb found the sensitive tip and circled it until it, too, grew hard.

"No." He groaned as if in pain and took his hand away.

Already alight with wanting Nick, Isabel didn't believe he didn't want her equally. She could already see the video in her mind's eye—her straddling him, riding him, brushing his chest with the tips of her breasts. He would take a tip in his mouth and suck the nipple into an exquisite point. Then he would take it between his fingers and pluck at it until she came. She closed her eyes and saw this as clearly as if it were on a television screen.

She rolled over and on top of Nick and straddled his thighs, where she pulled off her damp T-shirt and unhooked her bra.

"Isabel, don't do this."

"You don't really want me to stop."

She freed her breasts and leaned over, grazing his chest with her breasts just as she had seen in the video her mind had created. Her nipples were already hard. His erection came to life against her bottom and he took her in his mouth, rolled his tongue around the beaded nub exactly as she'd hoped he would. Isabel moaned with the pleasure.

Suddenly Nick rolled her and caught her under him, trapping her arms above her head. Remembering his comment about having control, she figured that's what he was about. Smiling, she wrapped her legs around his back and prepared herself for anything.

Except for his saying, "We can't do this anymore."

"We can't?" She moved her hips under him, stroked his erection to a new hardness. "I think we can. Maybe more than once."

Nick groaned and cursed. "Stop, please!"

He was serious!

Shocked, Isabel unhooked her legs and set him free. "What's wrong?"

"This is. I was."

"I don't understand."

Nick rolled off her and handed her the bra and T-shirt, which she hurriedly put on. He put his face in his hands and shook his head. Suddenly she felt sick inside and she didn't even know why.

"Nick, what's wrong?"

For a moment, she didn't think he was going to tell her.

Then he pulled his hands through his hair and said,

"I put this deal on the table—your having sex with me while we looked for Louise—thinking it would drive you away. I never thought you would take me up on it." He shook his head again. "But I was wrong to have done that to you, Isabel. Even though you agreed, I never should have let you go through with it. And you should never, ever let anyone make you sell yourself. There was a time when I had to do things…" He hesitated a moment, then continued, "I know what that feels like, and you're worth more than that. I apologize for making you compromise yourself. In the end, I'm no better than your father."

Nick's admission and apology stunned Isabel. He knew what it felt like? She closed her eyes. Dear Lord, he'd just been a boy….

More important to her was the main issue. He hadn't meant it…he was sorry…he feared she'd sold herself and not only to him. Nick's putting it that way horrified her…especially since she couldn't say he was wrong.

Her whole life had been one of compromise. Doing what was necessary politically to get the job done even if she didn't like it. Doing whatever her impassive father demanded of her to win his elusive love. Doing what Nick had required of her to get his help in finding Louise…

But had she *really* sold herself to Nick? Would she have slept with another man who'd demanded physical payment? The very thought repelled her. Isabel couldn't fathom doing so.

After all, this had been Nick Novak. Her first love. Her only love.

She'd blamed her father for her refusal to go to anyone else for help, but it had been she who had purposely sought out Nick. For, somewhere in the deep reaches of her soul, a light had beckoned in the darkness. A possibility. A chance for her to recapture something that had been precious to her.

She touched his shoulder and moved closer. At first he didn't move. Then, as if he couldn't help himself, he reached out, wrapped an arm around her, then lay back. She rested her head against his chest and listened to his heartbeat. The sound mesmerized her, and she felt as if she could lie there listening forever.

"I still want you, Nick," she whispered, fearing to say more, fearing to reveal how much she cared.

He pulled her closer and stroked her hair. "And I want you, Isabel. But not like this. Not here."

For the moment, she was content with that, with their wanting each other, with the secret of her love. And when they got back to the real world, she would prove to him that she was worthy of *his* love, too.

AN ELEVATED TRAIN OVERHEAD careened by the old redbrick warehouse, but it seemed to move silently through the night as the screech of metal on metal was drowned out by the techno-rock pouring from the entrance to the rave.

Nick anchored an arm around Isabel's waist as he handed the doorkeeper their entrance fee. No IDs required because no liquor was sold on the premises. What was likely being sold was far more dangerous.

"Whatever you do, stick to me like glue," he told Isabel.

''I can take care of myself.''

Actually, he wasn't sure she could. Danger could come from anywhere, and in this crowd…was a scream really a scream if it couldn't be heard?

She asked, ''How in the world are we going to find Louise in this?''

''This'' being a crush of bodies that extended wall-to-wall. Some were sitting in upholstered couches and chairs brought in for the occasion. Teens were doubling up, necking, doing other things in the dark, thick with smoke, things that their parents wouldn't like. Most were on the dance floor, gyrating up against one another. Raves were hotbeds for the sale of ecstasy, the drug that made a user crave closeness and the touch of another.

A thought that made Nick decidedly uncomfortable.

''We need to work our way through the dance floor,'' Isabel said directly in his ear.

The sensation sent a ripple effect straight down Nick's spine. Closeness with Isabel in this crowd couldn't be avoided. Torture that he'd brought on himself. ''Come on, then.''

As they cut to the middle of the dance floor, Nick kept an eye out for Louise and noted that Isabel was doing the same.

Finding an open spot, he stopped her. ''This'll do for a while. Dance and make it look convincing.''

As if anyone would notice what they were doing. The kids were into one another to the max. Girls slithering around the guys, guys boldly groping the girls.

While searching every face for one that belonged

to her sister, Isabel did a credible job of pretending
to dance. Her brushing up against him drove Nick
crazy.

It was best that everything was now out in the open
and he'd instigated his hands-off policy. Nick knew
that he didn't fit into Isabel's world—that is, her father's world—which meant they had no future. Better
to adjust to that truth now.

But, oh, how difficult it was to be with her, to be
so close that he could inhale her unique musk. To feel
her lush body brush up against his. He'd be walking
with a hard-on for days just remembering.

"Let's keep moving," he suggested, speaking directly into her ear. "That way, toward the staircase."

They inched through gyrating bodies rubbing up
against one another, but the sex spell began to wear
off...to be replaced by something else. Something
more insidious that raised the hair at the back of his
neck. The sensation that they were being watched.

But no matter how hard Nick scanned the area
around them, he couldn't discern by whom.

THE WAREHOUSE WAS HOT and Isabel was thirsty, so
she started making her way to the bar. Though Nick
came along without question, he seemed distracted,
undoubtedly on the lookout for her sister. Which was
just as well, Isabel thought, because the faster this was
over, the quicker she would be free of him.

You don't want that, a voice inside her head whispered. *You want him, now more than ever.*

Maybe she did, but she wasn't going to have him.
He'd set her straight on that count.

Besides, the only important thing was to find Louise—*if* she could find her in this ridiculous crush. She couldn't even get directly up to the bar. Kids were three deep in front of her.

"How do I get a drink?" she yelled.

"Magic," a big, good-looking charmer said. He reached through the crowd and pulled out a glass. "Magic punch, to be specific," he said, holding out a plastic cup of what looked like pale red liquid.

Nick swiped it right out of her hand. "The lady would like a club soda," he yelled.

But before the club soda came, Isabel was distracted by a flash of blond hair and a familiar face near the back wall.

"Louise!"

"You see her?"

"There!"

But even as Isabel pointed, the throng swallowed her sister. Panicked, she darted forward and clawed her way through hot, sweaty bodies.

"I think she went back toward that exit," she told Nick, who was directly behind her.

Her heart was racing frantically. *This is it! Don't let her get away!*

They reached the exit, which was open, letting in fresh air.

"Maybe she went out in the alley," Nick said, encircling her waist with his arm and pushing through the people blocking the open door.

"Stamp?" a guy with green hair asked. "You need one if you want back in."

"Yeah, sure," Nick said, holding out his hand but straining to get a look behind them.

What in the world was he looking for? Isabel wondered.

She got her hand stamped and left a distracted Nick behind, racing to catch up to Louise. A bunch of kids had come out into the alley to talk or to neck. Fearing her sister would be long gone, she was relieved to spot Louise leaning against a Dumpster, flirting with a boy.

Nick caught up to her just then. She gripped his arm but didn't say a word. He followed suit and pushed her forward. A glance back assured her that Nick meant to let her have some privacy.

She was only a few yards away when Louise looked up and directly at them. Her expression panicked, she tried to run, but the boy delayed her long enough for Isabel to catch up and grab her up in a big hug.

"Lulu, oh my God, you don't know how worried I've been about you."

She was gratified when the embrace was returned and relieved when the boy melted into the night.

"I'm sorry, Izzie." Under the glare of the alley lights, Louise's eyes were round and watery as if she wanted to cry. "I didn't mean to make you worry."

"It's over now." Isabel backed off but still held her sister lightly. "No more running. You'll come home with me and we'll fix whatever needs fixing."

"You can't fix it, Izzie. Even you can't change things, not this time," Louise said cryptically. "And I'm not coming home. I can't."

"Then we'll go to a hotel. I'll get us an apartment—"

"No!" Louise jerked away and ran.

"Wait!" Isabel yelled, following.

But a couple of guys stumbled into her path and one grabbed her around the waist and started dancing her around the alley.

"Don't let her get away!" she yelled to Nick.

Then out from the shadows came a black-clothed man, who grabbed Louise and pulled her into a gangway.

"Lulu!" Isabel screamed as Nick raced right by her in hot pursuit.

HE COULDN'T BELIEVE HE'D snatched the brat right out from under the bitch's nose.

"Let go of me!" Louise yelled, struggling. "Stop!"

He stopped long enough to backhand her into the brick wall. "Shut up or there will be more where that came from." Then he started up again, dragging her along.

"No!" she cried, not even trying to fight anymore. "I won't say anything—really, I won't. I promise! I won't even go home, not ever!"

"No, you *won't*," he said, running his thumb over the knife in his pocket. "Not ever."

13

NICK SHOT AROUND THE CORNER and saw Louise being dragged down the gangway.

"Stop!" he yelled as he pounded the pavement and quickly narrowed the distance between them. "The police are on their way!"

A lie, but one that tripped up the villain. He literally stumbled, and Louise took the opportunity to shove him against the brick wall. Before the bastard could regain the advantage, Nick was on him, grabbing him by the back of his collar and jerking him so hard that he let go of the girl completely. Tearing himself free of Nick's grip, he spun around.

Little light found its way into that section of the gangway, so the attacker's face was just barely visible, protected by a combination of the dark and the billed cap. He began to back away, a sharp click warning Nick of real trouble if he went after the bastard. No doubt he'd intended on using the switchblade to cut Louise.

And Isabel.

Remembering that the woman he loved might have died at the bastard's hands that morning, Nick saw red and went after him. He jumped back when he sensed more than saw the guy's knife hand lash out, then Nick quickly advanced once more.

Ready for the next thrust, he kicked out and made contact with bone.

"Damn!"

A clatter first against brick, then sidewalk, assured Nick the other man was disarmed.

He launched himself forward for a full body tackle and sent them both flying toward the street. They landed hard and went rolling, trading punches. Try as he might, he wasn't able to get a look at the other man's face. He did note they were a match in build and strength. He got the bastard in the gut, but still rolling, landed beneath his attacker.

"Nick!"

Isabel's scream from the gangway distracted him only for a second.

But that second was long enough to get his own face smashed. His head flew back and smacked the sidewalk. And in the moment he saw stars, the bastard flew to his feet, kicked Nick hard in the side and ran off.

"Nick!" Isabel screamed again as she popped out of the gangway.

He struggled to a sitting position with all intentions of getting up and following the villain. But as he made it to his feet, a frantic Isabel grabbed on to him.

"Louise! Where is she?"

Nick looked around only to realize that, once more, the teenager had disappeared.

"HOLD STILL," ISABEL DEMANDED as she swabbed the cut over Nick's eyebrow with hydrogen peroxide.

She was fighting the urge to take him into her arms and hold him.

"Aah!" He squeezed his eyes closed and ducked away from her hand. "Enough with the Florence Nightingale routine already."

"I still think you ought to let a doctor look at that," she said, watching the blood ooze into his eyebrow. Breathless with wanting to touch him, to make love to him, she somehow held herself back. "You need stitches."

"A couple of these strips will do."

Carefully, she taped the cut shut, then cleaned up the blood. "What if you have a concussion?"

"Look into my eyes," Nick said, his voice silky smooth and laden with suggestion.

"This is no time for joking."

Thankfully, his pupils looked evenly dilated.

Isabel swallowed hard. How could he joke at a time like this, anyway? First she'd been freaked by Louise's disappearance and then she'd gotten a good look at his face. Pleas to go to an ER had gotten her nowhere, but at least he'd agreed to go back to his place where she could treat his injuries.

Finishing her attempt at first aid, she said, "You'll probably live."

"Disappointed?"

"You've never given me a reason to be disappointed, Nick." Other than when he'd turned her down earlier, which was no doubt the reason every square inch of her felt on fire now. Washing her hands in the bathroom sink, she thought about how she was to blame for his being hurt. "I'm the one—"

"Stop." He grabbed her arm and turned her to face him. "Neither of us is to blame here."

Then why was she feeling so guilty?

"I'm going to make that call now," she choked out.

After all that had happened, they'd agreed to call the authorities. Even so, Isabel had insisted on giving her father a heads up. But that seemed to be impossible when he didn't answer his cell phone. She could only imagine why….

Hanging up, she said, "My father's not answering. We'll have to wait awhile longer to bring in the police."

Nick crossed his arms over his chest. "We shouldn't have waited this long."

He didn't ask again, but the unspoken question about what she'd been hiding lay between them. Gathering her courage, Isabel decided that it was now or never.

Taking a deep breath, she said, "It's time I told you everything, Nick."

As she should have from the beginning. Instead, she'd made him prove that he was worthy of her trust, though almost getting himself killed had been overkill. How could she have let things go this far without confiding in him?

"So you swear to tell the truth, the whole truth and nothing but the truth?" he asked.

Let him be amused now. Once he knew, he would be anything but.

"The bathroom's not the place to discuss this. Let's go in the other room."

"Too confining in here?"

Nick moved close enough to make her blood boil over. Ready to melt, she remembered that he'd called a halt to their deal, and she wasn't sure where or when he would be ready to pick up. Slipping by him, glad to be free of the small space and be back in his studio, she hugged herself, willed herself to stop wanting what she couldn't have at the moment.

The first thing she laid her eyes on was his trundle bed. Averting her gaze, she went to the window and looked down on the street. Even though the hour was late, Friday night brought the pub crawlers, so plenty of people were still out and about.

"Would it be easier if you took the hot seat?" Nick asked.

Hot. Wanting in the worst way to remove her clothing, to have nothing touching her skin but him, Isabel turned toward Nick. He indicated the stool and camera still set up as it had been the other day.

Remembering all the video fantasies of them making love that she'd been having, flushing at the memory of actually being recorded in a sexual encounter, she wondered why he would want to tape her now.

"I think I'll just stay right here."

"Fine." Nick joined her, opened the window next to her and took a seat on the sill. "So spill."

"The night before Louise disappeared, she stayed out far past her curfew," Isabel began, rubbing at her own arms. "My father waited up for her and they had a row. I heard them arguing, but I was in bed, so I couldn't hear what they were saying. The next morning I went to Louise's room to talk to her. She'd been increasingly at odds with Dad, getting into trouble, and I wanted to find out why. She was gone. She'd left me a note saying she wouldn't be back. Then I went to Dad, but he refused to elaborate on their argument...not until she actually had been gone for twenty-four hours and no one I called had seen her.''

''And then the senator told you...what?''

''That Louise said she'd come to the office looking for him and had heard his voice through the back door. She'd followed it upstairs where she'd caught him with another woman.'' Such a scandal could bring down her father's career if news got to the media, the voters being intolerant of infidelity in their public servants. ''Apparently, he's been keeping this Amber Bower for years.''

''And just upstairs from his office,'' Nick mused. ''How convenient for long lunches.''

It made her wonder if that's where her father actually went when he said he was meeting with his constituents. Isabel shook her head in disgust.

''So you knew about this?'' Nick asked.

''Not before, no. My father isn't perfect, but I had no idea that he was morally bankrupt.'' Or that he would ever ask her to compromise herself to cover it up, the heart of her own dilemma. ''I used to wonder why he and Mother spent so little time together. She always said that he had his life and she had hers and that she was perfectly satisfied with things the way they were.''

"What does she say now that Louise is on the streets?"

"She's concerned, of course, but she's not what you would call a strong woman. She's never been able to handle Louise. She has always left that to me."

"What a pair your parents make."

"Yes, well…"

She closed her eyes for a moment and the emotions welled in her, threatening to spill over. She hugged herself, tried to make herself feel better. But the void seemed unending, as if something was irreparably split open in her. The lack of connection to loved ones would never let her feel whole.

When she opened her eyes, Nick was staring up at her, his expression thoughtful. "So your sister ran because she found out your father has a mistress."

"Apparently."

"Does that make sense to you? I mean Louise temporarily running away because she was shocked and her world was turned upside down is one thing. But vowing never to come back? And then there's the matter of the mysterious stalker who wants to kill you both. There's got to be more. What aren't you telling me, Isabel?"

"Nothing. I promise I'm not holding anything back. That's all I know about it."

"Then maybe the senator hasn't told you everything."

She nodded. "I came to the same conclusion myself. But what more could there be? What could Louise know that someone would kill to keep secret?"

"And how did he know where to find either of you?"

A rapid pulse beat in Isabel's throat. Trying to catch her breath, she forced out the words. "The cell phone. My father wanted me to check in."

"I'll bet he did. So you called him and told him where we were?" Nick asked tightly.

"I told him about Club Undercover," she admitted. "And about the rave."

The obscenity that came from Nick's mouth was enough to make a sailor blush.

"My father is no murderer," she insisted.

"Perhaps not directly," he agreed. "The guy I waltzed with tonight was my size and strong. Probably around my age. So who fitting that description would have a motive?"

"Maybe one of the men working for him..."

"Why?"

"I don't have a clue."

"How about on the senator's orders?" Nick suggested. "Otherwise, how would the bastard know where to find you or Louise?"

Isabel felt herself crumbling from the inside out. Normally, she could put up a good front, not let anyone know her true feelings. But she'd run out of whatever it took to keep up appearances. She wanted Nick to hold her and reassure her. Her body clamored for it.

"You're saying you think our father wants Louise and me dead?"

She blinked and tears coursed down her cheeks. The thought was too much for her to bear. The possibility that her world was turning upside down…she didn't know what was wrong with her. She'd never felt so…so needy.

Before she could get herself under control, Nick had her in his arms and was kissing her forehead. Isabel clung to him, shuddering with something akin to grief. The death of a dream was nothing to take lightly.

"You were right, you know. I've always done everything my father expected of me. I've tried everything to please him. To be the son he never had."

"You wanted him to show that he loved you."

"Pitiful, isn't it?"

Gone were the hopes she had for her future. Gone was the image of her father gazing at her with pride in his eyes at her accomplishments. Gone. All gone.

"I feel like such a child," she whispered.

The tears were coming faster now. She slashed at them with a shaky hand until Nick wiped them away for her and said, "I think every child wants his or her parents' love, no matter our age."

Isabel knew he, too, had been denied that.

"Father has always had my loyalty, even when I've seen his negative side. But this…it was too much for me to swallow and excuse. I didn't know what to do, Nick. I had to find Louise, and until then, I didn't want to think about anything else. My father has done so many good things for people, I didn't want to be too hasty to cast judgment on him and open up his private transgressions to the world, too."

"Because you still have faith that the world is basically a fair and good place."

"Someday, I'll get over my naiveté."

"I hope not totally," Nick said. "Despite current proof to the contrary, the world has a lot of fair and good people."

"Like whom?"

"Gideon. Jerry Kramer. You."

"Me?" Isabel stared up at Nick, her breath ragged. "I thought you didn't much care for me."

When he said, "I care for you, Isabel, more than you know," her pulse sped up.

"Nick...?"

"Shh."

When he shushed her, his face was so close to hers that she could feel his warm breath lave her cheek. Her heart thudded harder. He cared for her, despite the past.

Isabel blinked, and when a single final tear splashed her cheek, Nick quickly kissed it away.

Before she knew what was happening, his mouth was covering hers, and he was kissing her the way she'd dreamed of for years after he'd gone. She kissed him back with equal parts of passion...and love.

Of course, she had loved Nick always. Without that subconscious certainty, she couldn't have given herself to him with such abandon. No, truthfully, she wouldn't have done so at all.

Now it seemed that Nick felt the same way about her, and suddenly the burden she'd been carrying grew lighter. Despite the seriousness of their situation, the fact that Louise was still on the run and Isabel didn't know why, her spirit lifted and she felt almost giddy with relief. It didn't make sense—someone had tried to murder her that very morning and undoubtedly would have murdered Louise tonight—but suddenly she felt better than she had for days.

When Nick ended the kiss, he pressed his forehead to hers and clasped her head with both hands so that she couldn't move away from him. Not that she was eager to.

He said, "I've been wanting to do that all night."

"Kiss me?" She was so giddy, laughter bubbled up, just waiting to be released. "I thought all you were interested in was having your needs met."

"So I needed to be kissed," he admitted. "The sex was great, but...mmm...the sex was *really* great."

The change in his tone nearly took away her breath. She tried to get closer, imagined she could get inside of him if she tried. "You sound as if you might regret having stopped."

"I have my memories to keep me warm." He grinned at her. "And, uh, there's always the videotape."

The word dropped like a sexual landmine between them.

"The videotape." Wide-eyed, she pulled her head free and remembered her video fantasy. "How many women have you taped?"

"I don't know. I've lost count of my subjects over the years."

She swallowed hard and all the little video clips she'd dreamed up came flashing through her head, but rather than seeing herself, she imagined him with numerous faceless women.

"So this is a regular thing for you?" she asked sadly.

"Video is my business, remember."

"Well, yes, but I didn't know you were into X-rated stuff."

Nick laughed. "You do have a naughty imagination. That's one of the things I like about you."

"Are you saying you don't do pornos?"

He laughed harder and shook his head. "Sorry to disappoint you. Only that one the other day."

Laughter exploded from her, as well, and amusing as her suppositions might have been, Isabel felt herself grow hot with embarrassment.

But when the laughter died, she thought about the consequences. About what would happen later, after they went to the authorities, after Louise was safe. She didn't see how any of that would be kept out of the media. How Nick would be, and what he did for a living. What if the wrong people somehow got their hands on that tape?

Sobering, she said, "Maybe we ought to erase the tape."

Nick's eyebrows shot up. "Without even watching it? Are you sure that's what you want?"

When he put it like that...

Isabel had to admit to a certain curiosity. "Watching first wouldn't hurt."

Watching might even inspire Nick, she decided, more than anything wanting to lose herself in him again, especially now that she knew he cared.

"I suppose from a professional point of view, you

might want to check out the results of your experiment.''

His eyes narrowed to slits. ''Absolutely.''

Without saying a word, he drew her toward the other side of the room. He stopped at the stool and made her sit. Then he flipped a switch.

The monitor came on and there she was, big as life. She couldn't stop from watching herself unbutton her blouse. Heat flushed through her as his hands slid around her neck, between her breasts, then lifted them…

This was better than any video in her imagination!

Isabel squirmed in her seat, her eyes glued to the monitor. The way Nick's hands were touching her breasts…she could almost feel them on her sensitive flesh now. Her nipples pebbled and a slow, syrupy sensation invaded her thighs and the soft flesh between them.

The desire that had been plaguing her since she set eyes on him the other day multiplied.

''So what do you think?'' he murmured, his lips directly next to her ear.

The only thing she could think about was having more… Only this time it would be different because they wouldn't have to guard their feelings any longer. They would be making love, not simply having sex.

She stared at the monitor, but the fun had ended—the Isabel on the screen was composed, readying herself to leave.

She looked to Nick, who was staring at her. The *real* her.

"I think it was too short," she said softly. "Maybe you should play it again."

Nick moved to the equipment rack and made some adjustments until her image appeared on the screen once more. "I have a better idea."

This was live, not tape, for the image wore a T-shirt and jeans and was a study in shadow—no grid lights to illuminate every detail this time, but the camera was sensitive enough to pick up plenty.

"What are you doing?" she asked, noting the camera's red light once again glaring at her.

Moving back toward her, Nick pulled off his T-shirt and unsnapped his jeans. "Only what you like."

His torso was beautiful, all trim muscle, his abs a rippled wonder to behold. She hadn't really been able to see him in the dark reaches they'd invaded the last two nights, and now she couldn't stop looking. When he slipped behind her, she glanced at the monitor and was disappointed that he all but disappeared from the screen.

"Take off your T-shirt," he whispered.

"No, *you* do it."

He didn't argue. Encircling her waist with his hands, he bunched up the material and inched it slowly, sensuously out of the jeans. The tiny movements teased her flesh and a tingling discomfort spread downward to her toes, so that she kicked off her shoes and managed to rid herself of her socks, as well.

"That's better," she said with a sigh.

"Is it?"

"My skin feels like it's on fire." Isabel widened her eyes and blinked her lashes at him provocatively. "Oh. What can be done about that?"

"Let's see if I can help," Nick offered.

His hands disappeared under the cloth, and she couldn't see him undoing her jeans or touching her flesh on the monitor. What she could see was a man in control, his expression so intense that it held her in its grip.

His fingers spread along her ribs. She watched his nostrils flare and raised her arms over her head so that she could hook her hands behind his neck. Her breasts lifted visibly beneath the thin material and his hands followed.

The camera lens caught the way his expression went taut and his jaw tightened and she noticed him duck a hand behind her, heard the zipper and the soft sound as his jeans fell to the floor. Both hands on her again, he stepped out of the jeans and pressed against her back.

Isabel closed her eyes for a moment and let the sensation of him stroking her breasts roll over her. The next thing she knew, the T-shirt lifted until the material tangled around her arms. He left it there as he removed her bra, exposing her breasts to the air.

While she struggled to free herself of the cotton trapping her, he cupped her flesh and thumbed her nipples into turgid peaks. She moaned, and with a gesture of triumph, threw the thing off. The second she lowered her arms, Nick bit the soft spot between her neck and shoulder, making her arch higher.

Eyes half-shut but still focused on the monitor, she

watched his hands and the wonderful things they were doing to her breasts as he rhythmically squeezed their fullness and thumbed her nipples.

Too turned-on to sit still, she inched back on the stool seat and pressed up against him. Hard as a rock, he shifted his erection along her denim-covered buttocks until it nestled in the crack.

The next thing she knew, one of his hands dipped low along her stomach, disappearing into her jeans. Her thighs spread in response and his fingers dipped into the waiting wetness. He slid one finger against her clit and farther back until he was inside her. She was moving now and couldn't stop.

"That's it, ride me, Isabel," Nick murmured in her hair as he inserted a second finger and twisted through her creamy wetness. "Ride me hard. I want to watch you. The way you move…your expression…so hot."

He was moving, too, behind her. But all she could see on the monitor was herself—a wanton—as she bucked harder and faster. Pressure mounted but she couldn't get high enough, fast enough.

"Come for me," Nick whispered in her ear, then bit down on her neck, the sensation zapping her right to her center.

She bucked high into him, pressing against his hand, still trapped in her jeans, his fingers deep inside her as waves of pleasure rolled through her.

She came back down with a round of soul-searing shudders.

Nick held her until she quieted, kissing her hair, her ear, her forehead.

Then he pulled his hand free and spun her stool

around so that she was facing him. Then he kissed her as if he were fucking her, his tongue hard and plunging deep. She found his cock with one hand and worked it in the same rhythm as the kiss. He was hard and hot and his head was wet with pre-come. He vibrated against her hand. She knew if they kept this up, he would come, and fast.

But that's not what she wanted. She wanted him inside her. She wanted them to be locked together in passion and love until they both fell, exhausted and sated.

As if he sensed her need, he pulled back and, hooking his hands in the back of her jeans and panties, jerked them down, exposing her derriere.

She let go of him and balanced herself on the stool with both hands while he tugged the garments out from under her. She spread her thighs to welcome him. He scooped both hands under her and lifted so that he could aim his head at her wet entrance.

"Now!" she urged, and he plunged in deep.

Finding her mouth again, he renewed the rhythm so that every part of her was assaulted at once. She lifted higher so that he could go deeper, and when he thrust in to the hilt, she lifted her legs and wrapped them around his waist.

Nick lifted her into his arms, and for a moment she was suspended, dancing on his cock, grasping him around the shoulders to stay on the ride. He turned until her back slammed against a wall.

"Now!" she urged again.

"Wait."

He groaned and shoved a hand between them, his

middle finger finding her clit and stroking. She arched against him and felt the tension spiral out of control.

He felt it, too.

"Now!" he growled.

Several thrusts and he began to quake, then his hot come jetted into her as she came with him.

Nick dropped his head to her shoulder, and Isabel wrapped her arms around him and clung tight as they shuddered together in completion.

When her heart rate settled, she murmured, "I love you, Nick. I've always loved you."

14

NICK WAITED UNTIL ISABEL was fast asleep on the trundle bed before kissing her on the forehead, rising and taking his clothes into the bathroom. There he made a quick phone call to Nate Bishop before getting dressed.

Nick knew he should have done this once he'd figured out that Lulu and Louise were the same girl. Forget the street code of honor he'd warned Isabel about when they'd begun their odyssey—once she learned that he'd been holding out on her, she might never forgive him.

Taking one last look at the woman he loved, Nick stole out of the studio without making a sound but for the soft click of the door and the snap of the lock behind him. He would be back before she awoke, hopefully with everything she needed to make her happy.

The street was nearly deserted and he waited at the door. Five minutes later, a loud buzz alerted him to Nate's arrival. Nate Bishop, his landlord and Annie's new love, to the rescue.

"Thanks for coming so fast," Nick said.

Nate got off the Harley and handed Nick the helmet. "Bring the hog back in one piece, would you?"

"Keep my woman in one piece while I'm gone and it's a deal."

Nate saluted him. "I will sit on these stairs and keep watch until you return."

Grateful, for Nick wouldn't have been okay with leaving Isabel alone after what she'd been through, he said, "I owe you one."

This wasn't the first time Nate had come through for him recently—on Annie's urging, he'd given Nick the keys to the abandoned building owned by his company, Cornerstone Realty, the place where Nick had taken Isabel the first night. Even though he'd threatened her with the streets, he'd cheated to make sure she remained safe.

After hopping on the Harley, Nick headed for Humboldt Park, his thoughts filled with Isabel, his woman...but would she be once she knew?

Not more than five minutes later, he slowed the motorcycle and parked it in front of a gray-stone building that had once been the home of some wealthy industrialist. Luckily, lights still shone through the leaded-glass-trimmed windows. And, thankfully, the middle-aged woman who answered the door was someone he knew.

"Nick, what in the world are you doing here so late? It's after midnight!"

"I've got a serious situation, Marlene. A kid who's in real danger."

She looked out to the street. "Where?"

"Hopefully, here." He'd suspected as much the night before when Isabel had found the phone number in the shed. "A pretty blonde who goes by the name of Lulu."

Marlene nodded and stood back. "Come on in. You know it's up to her whether or not she wants to talk to you."

"Tell her it's life or death."

Marlene gaped but quickly recovered. "A-all right. I'll be right back."

She shot up the staircase as fast as any kid and Nick paced the common room, empty at this hour. Only one lamp was lit low, and it threw the room into deep shadows.

He hadn't known Louise was here for sure, but would Isabel ever believe him? And even if he had known, he couldn't have brought her here, couldn't have revealed Louise's safe house. Protecting these kids was part of the code he lived by. If he betrayed her, word would get round, then no kid would ever trust him again. And that would be the end of the good he could do for them.

He was caught between a rock and a hard place—unless Louise was ready to talk to Isabel, his hands were tied.

As good as her word, Marlene came back quickly, indicated the staircase and hurried to the back of the building. Louise stood there, staring at him.

"I need to talk to you."

She came all the way downstairs but appeared reluctant and somewhat distrustful. Her gaze quickly swept every corner of the room.

"I'm alone," he assured her.

"Why were you with Isabel tonight?"

So she had seen him. Nick hadn't been sure. "It's a long story." One that Isabel could relate if she wanted. "The crux of the matter is that she wanted me to help find you."

"And you didn't bring her here."

"That would be against the rules. You know that. It's up to you now, Louise."

"What's up to me?"

"To turn yourself in. To Isabel."

She was already shaking her head. "I can't."

"Why can't you?" When she refused to answer, he said, "Isabel is out of her mind with worry over you. She won't stop until she finds you. Unless something happens to you first. Like tonight…"

He was leaving the door open for her to spill, to tell him something, anything, about why she'd been dragged off. He considered telling her about the bastard trying to murder Isabel, but he didn't think that would be a good idea at the moment. He might scare off the kid for good.

"Some guy grabbing me isn't going to change my mind."

"Some guy?" Again he waited, but Louise was as stubborn as her older sister. "So, you're not in danger, right? And neither is Isabel?"

Her eyes widened a fraction. "Isabel?"

He nodded. "Right. Whoever grabbed you tonight got a good look at her." When that brought no response, he changed gears. "Your sister is at my place for the night. She would be so relieved to see you and talk to you about whatever is troubling you."

Louise shook her head and backed off toward the staircase. "I can't go back."

"Not back. To Isabel. She needs you." And as she hurried up the stairs to be swallowed by the dark at the top, he added, "If you change your mind, you know where to find her, at least for now."

Cursing, Nick ran a hand through his hair. Still nothing from the kid that would give him hope.

What the hell was he supposed to do next?

So WHAT THE HELL WAS THE GUY in the black leather doing in the building? he wondered. Were Mr. Hog and Novak a tag team with Isabel? Did she do them one at a time or both together?

Not that he cared—just curiosity born of boredom.

Feeling his energy waning, he popped another pill. He had to stay awake. He had to see this through. One pill left. He'd better save it in case he needed it later. Should have taken more from his stash. In a few minutes, he would be flying, able to handle anything.

And Isabel would be so damn easy. She'd welcome him inside, would maybe even cry on his shoulder. Tell him about what happened to her in the park district locker room that morning.

He laughed.

Sweet. That's what it would be. He'd made some mistakes, but no more. He couldn't afford to, not when the list was getting longer. Now he not only had to get rid of the brat and Isabel, he'd have to see to Novak, as well. The last would be a pleasure, he decided, as his side twitched, reminding him why.

So what was the Hell's Angels wanna-be doing there? Was he up in his office at this time of night?

He'd figured Isabel and Novak would come back to the building eventually, so he'd made it his business to case the building over the past few days when he wasn't tied up with business or chasing after Louise. That was why he'd recognized the guy when he'd removed the helmet.

If he was going to make his move on Isabel, he needed to do it now. He got out of the car. He'd been sitting here for hours, since before Isabel and Novak had come back, so it took a minute to get the kinks out.

He stretched his limbs and crossed the street on an angle, casually heading for the doorway. Not many cars this time of the morning.

No witnesses. That was good.

His adrenaline kicked in, and so did the drug. His pulse quickened as did his pace. He wanted to get in and get it over with before Novak returned. Then he would wait and take care of that Novak bastard who'd blown his plans for the night.

Almost there. One foot in front of the other. Quick look around to make sure he was alone.

He approached the doorway…started to reach out… and then swept his hand up to his hair and kept walking.

"Damn!" he growled. "Damn, damn, damn!"

Just as he'd been about to reach for the door, he'd seen him reclining in his leather on the bottom stairs. Mr. Hog hadn't gone up to his office, after all.

Would nothing ever go right?

"Nick?" Isabel felt his absence the moment she awoke. "Nick, where are you?"

Sliding her legs over the edge of the trundle bed, she yawned and found the top sheet, which she wrapped around herself. Where was he? Had he fallen asleep in a chair?

She rose, flipped on a light and quickly surveyed the studio. No Nick at all. Where could he have gone after midnight?

Restless, she wandered around his studio, touching the equipment, considering what a turn-on watching them make love had been.

From the looks of the equipment, Nick had a lot of money invested here. Look how far the kid who'd spent time on the streets had come, she thought. Wondering how he'd gotten himself on the right track, she was also curious about the documentary he was making. His personal project. She couldn't wait to see it completed.

Isabel glanced at the rack of tapes, all labeled, most with a single name: Missy, Chica, Glory. Considering *those* names, she might question the contents—wonder if they weren't home-shot pornography, after all—if the tapes next to them weren't labeled Kyle and Eugene and Norman. So many runaways, she thought, yawning again and starting to turn away.

That's when she saw it, the one name guaranteed to jump out at her and grab her by the throat.

Lulu.

She froze and her pulse began to pound. No, it couldn't be.

But instinct told her it *could*…

She had to see for herself.

Somehow, shaking hands or not, Isabel managed to turn on the equipment and insert the tape into the VCR. Throat tight, she watched the screen as the camera adjusted and a shot of a young blonde came into focus.

"Louise!" she whispered.

"What should I talk about?" came the familiar voice from the speakers.

"Anything you want. Your experiences on the street. How you're getting along. What needs to happen before you go home."

Louise's expression darkened. *"I can't go home. Nothing is like it seemed. It's all a lie. Everything I believed in is a lie."*

"There's no one for you?"

"My sister. But she doesn't know..."

Isabel's stomach knotted and she had trouble breathing as the full extent of Nick's perfidy hit her.

"Your sister doesn't know what?"

"She's not who she thinks she is. And she's not the only one." Louise shook her head. *"Can we start over?"*

"Sure, if you like—"

"Can we start over?"

It took Isabel a moment to realize the last came from behind her. Stopping the tape, she stood staring at the television screen and listened to the sound of her heart drumming furiously through her ears.

"Isabel, I didn't know, not at first," Nick said. "She called herself Lulu. You called her Louise."

Isabel turned toward him. "You've known long

enough.'' Though covered by a sheet, she felt utterly exposed. "Why didn't you tell me, Nick?"

"I couldn't—"

"Couldn't or wouldn't?" The drumbeat in her ears competed with her words. "You've been playing a damn game with me—"

"This is no game."

Rising, she stalked over to gather her clothes from the floor. "I thought you were actually trying to help me find her."

"I was."

She went around him but he followed her to the bathroom. She slammed the door in his face. Shaking with fury and betrayal, she dressed as fast as she could.

Nick Novak, the one man she thought she could trust, had made a damn fool of her. If he had told her he knew Louise, it would have been over too quickly for him. He couldn't have given her those streetwise lessons on living the life of a runaway. He wouldn't have had his opportunity to use her.

She'd thought he cared for her. Loved her, even.

Well, wasn't she the biggest fool on earth!

The moment she opened the door, Nick ambushed her. "I keep the confidence of the kids I tape—or help. You knew that because I told you up-front! It's part of the code, keeping confidences—you, of all people, should understand that concept since you do it for your father. Isn't that what this whole thing between us is about?"

She pushed by him. How dare he have the audacity

to look angry, as if she was the one who'd done something wrong?

She stood in the middle of his studio, gawking as if looking for something to collect. But she had nothing but the clothes on her back.

She didn't even have him.

About to leave, Isabel hesitated when he said, "As much as I wanted to, I couldn't tell you what I knew."

"How much *do* you know?" she demanded. From his tight-lipped expression, Isabel was certain there was more. "You know where Louise is, don't you? You've known all along."

"No, not all along. Not until tonight."

"Humboldt House."

"Yeah, Humboldt House."

"Where is it? What's the address?"

"I can't tell you."

"But Louise *is* there, right? And that's where you were just now? You went to...what? Warn her I was getting close?"

He didn't answer and she wanted to hit him. Even now he wouldn't be straight with her.

"I never would have thought it of you, Nick." Her throat was so thick she had to force out the words. "Congratulations. I guess we're finally even for what I did to you in high school."

With that, she headed for the door.

"Isabel, that isn't fair! Wait a minute! You can't leave now—"

"Just watch me!" she shouted back. "And, uh, oh yeah—I never want to see you again!"

Running down the stairs, she tried playing the game. The one where she blocked everything out and presented a cool, clean facade, as if she hadn't a care in the world. But by the time she hit the street, she was struggling to keep from losing it.

Eyes stinging, only her will keeping her together, Isabel stood at the doorway, the realization that she had no money hitting her. The bank across the six corners—it must have an ATM. She could get cash and then find a taxi.

As she headed that way, she automatically scanned her surroundings. Not much on the streets. Two cars coming through the intersection. A lone taxi going the other way—empty. A truck at a red light. A young exec-type who'd had too much to drink weaving his way home.

Then movement caught her eye—racing down Milwaukee, a slight figure, pale hair standing out under the streetlights.

The product of wishful thinking or could it be...?

"Lulu!" she called, waving.

The head bobbed up and found her. The girl waved and yelled, "Izzie!" the nickname nearly drowned out by an engine starting up behind Isabel.

Louise ran to the intersection where she had to wait for the truck to pass. Isabel reached the crossroads just as a car came screeching away from a curb along Damen Avenue. Expecting it to stop at the red light, she was horrified when the vehicle seemed to pick up speed as it turned, and an impatient Louise stepped off the curb before the light changed.

"Louise, watch it!" Isabel yelled as the vehicle made a wide arc.

Louise looked up just in time—the car was speeding straight for her. The teenager swerved off to her right and jumped back up on the curb, safe by mere inches. The car continued to pick up speed and careered down Milwaukee.

For a moment, heart pounding, torn between imagination and reality, Isabel stared after the speeding vehicle. Had the driver purposely tried to hit Louise or not?

Quickly crossing the street, Louise was all over her, enveloping her in a big hug. "Oh, Izzie, I'm so glad to see you!"

Isabel hugged her back, but she was distracted, still watching, waiting for the car to swing around and come back for them both. But the street remained quiet but for the few vehicles passing at a reasonable speed.

Isabel brought her attention back to her sister. "We have to go home, Lulu."

The teenager appeared horrified. "No, I can't live with Daddy anymore!"

"I'll make other arrangements for us, I promise, but we have to get off the streets to someplace safe." She would warn her father in person, but if he wasn't there, too bad, she had to call the police. "We can get a good night's sleep, then in the morning, pack and move to a hotel until I can find us an apartment—"

"No!" Louise pulled herself out of Isabel's arms. "You don't understand."

"What don't I understand, Lulu? I know about Amber Bower."

"And our brother—do you know about him, too?"

"Brother?" The air whooshed out of Isabel's chest. She had a brother?

"Half brother, and he's turned out to be a bastard for real! He's the one who grabbed me last night."

Unable to connect with the new information, Isabel felt as if her mind was racing out of control. "We can't talk about it here." She looked around. Where the hell was a taxi when you really needed one? "We have to get someplace safe!"

Grabbing Louise's hand, she started pulling her back along Damen toward the rapid-transit station. Maybe they could duck under the turnstiles and get to a train.

"I'm not going home."

"Fine. I get it."

She got lots of things now. Her mind reeled with Louise's revelation.

"Why can't we just go into Nick's place?"

"Nick's place?" Of course Louise knew where to find him—it seemed all the kids on the street did. "Not an option."

"I—I don't understand. Isn't that where you just came from? He said you were there when he tried to get me to come back with him to see you."

Yards from the rapid-transit station, Isabel stopped. "What? That's what Nick was doing tonight?"

"He couldn't bring you to see me, because that would have been against the house rules. And no one would have ever trusted him again. But he came to tell me you were scared for me and needed me.''

"Oh, honey, you know I need you."

Isabel swept Louise into her arms and felt her sister shudder. Dear Lord, the hell she must have been through.

"I need you, too, Izzie."

"Now, isn't this touching."

The familiar voice drove an icy coldness through Isabel and she immediately whipped around, placing herself between Louise and the man she'd thought of as her friend, her buddy, the brother she'd never had.

Irony was no stranger to her tonight.

Trying to formulate an escape plan, Isabel grew very centered as she stared at him. He wasn't himself. His hair was a mess, matted and poking every which way. His eyes were big and staring and he didn't seem too steady on his feet.

Ignoring Louise's frantic poking and prodding her from behind, she calmly asked, "What are you doing here, Boyd? Isn't it above and beyond duty to report for work at this hour?''

His laugh sounded bitter. "I thought a family get-together was in order."

"Really, we don't have time," she said, subtly pushing her sister and inching toward the rapid-transit station. "Louise needs her rest."

"I insist you make time, Isabel."

With that, Boyd Cummings pulled out a gun.

IT HADN'T TAKEN NICK LONG to decide to call 911. He'd seen the sisterly reunion from his window and made the decision that it was time they let the authorities in on what had gone on. With both sisters there, the police would get the full story.

If Isabel had been mad enough to never want to see him again before, she was going to want to kill him now for taking things into his own hands, he thought, racing down the stairs two at a time. Nevertheless, he would see that the sisters stuck around until the police arrived. It was for their own good.

Only by the time he got out on the street, they were gone from the corner. He stared in that direction for a moment before turning to look behind him. He got a glimpse of Isabel and Louise before they disappeared from sight, followed by a familiar, ominous figure.

"Damn!"

He ran after them, slowing when he got to the break between buildings where he'd seen them disappear.

Cautiously, he peered around the corner. They'd gotten to the end of the station building and the bastard was waving a gun at them, pushing them back farther, directly under the elevated structure.

Nick's pulse pounded as he realized what was happening.

The area back there was deserted, private. And "L" trains pulling into stations and braking could be loud enough to cover some unusual noises…like gunshots.

Unless he thought of something, Nick feared both Isabel and Louise would be dead before the police got there.

"I DON'T UNDERSTAND WHAT'S going on," Isabel said, not liking the dark, dangerous-looking place littered with all sorts of refuse.

The only light came from the elevated platform above, cutting through the tracks and raining down on them in narrow ribbons.

"He's nuts, that's what," Louise said hotly. "Ever since I found out the truth, he's been threatening me to keep quiet."

Isabel gave her a nudge and a look that told her to keep her mouth shut now. Louise crossed her arms over her chest and got that stubborn expression that drove Mother crazy.

"Little Nancy Drew here couldn't leave it alone," Boyd said. "She was at Mama for details until she lost her temper and gave it to the kid straight. Then Louise came after *me* for not telling you both who I was."

"So we know who you are, so what?" Isabel asked, still not wanting to believe any of it.

"The brat's going to ruin everything for me," he said, staring at Louise. "Everything I've worked for all these years. You have no idea of what it's been like, being the ignored bastard son."

"I think I get the ignored part."

Boyd shook his head, and there was a wild look in his eyes when he said, "You two were recognized as his daughters, while I, his son, had to hide my identity."

"For the good of Father's political career."

If Boyd hadn't tried to kill her, if he wasn't holding that gun on her now, Isabel would feel sorry for him.

As it was, she knew how dangerous he could be and knew she had to figure out a way to neutralize him.

"But Father didn't ignore you completely," she said. "Obviously he wanted you near him. Otherwise he wouldn't have given you a job as a press liaison."

"Subordinate to you!" Boyd spat, obviously insulted by the fact. "Day after day, I had to pretend to be your friend, to be fond of the brat—"

"To what end, Boyd?" Isabel asked softly, trying her best to sound reasonable. And sane. "What's the bottom line here?"

"A smooth entry into the club, of course. With Senator William Grayson backing me, I plan a meteoric rise straight to the top of the Democratic party."

"President? Of the United States? You see yourself as presidential material?"

"Why not? I've got the looks for it. The charm. The connections. And obviously I'm good at waiting for what I want."

Either Boyd was delusional or…he was delusional. The only real question was whether he'd always thought this way or if drugs had influenced him. Now Isabel could see it—wild-eyed and nervously handling that gun, Boyd had to be on something.

"Actually, your deaths will give me that exposure I need," he continued. "Consoling the senator…getting on the gun-control wagon." He brightened. "That's it. I'll make that my platform for my first election—"

"You're insane!" Louise blurted out.

"No, no, I'm being ironic." Boyd laughed and

looked even more manic, if that were possible. "You want to know the real irony, Isabel? I'll be consoling him about your death to the whole world...and the senator's not even your father."

"Liar!" Louise shouted.

"Oh, he's *your* father, brat, just not *hers.*"

In a night of shocks, this outdid them all, Isabel thought. Her father not her father? That couldn't be true.

Boyd went on. "His marriage to your mother was a matter of convenience for them both. She got the father she needed for you, and he got her family's money and political backing for his career."

Noting a movement in the shadows behind him, Isabel tried to stay focused, saying, "I don't believe you."

"Ask him. Ask how he went into the marriage refusing to give up my mother. Another irony? She found out she was pregnant with me the day my father and your mother married. You do know they eloped. Oh, so romantic, right? That's so he wouldn't have to spend too much time with her. He spent his wedding night in *my* mother's bed."

Isabel's stomach twisted at the thought. She looked beyond him briefly to the moving shadows. Her blinking a few times turned the shifting dark shape back there into a Nick Novak facsimile. But that couldn't actually *be* Nick. He was out of her life for good.

Or was he?

Realizing she wasn't imagining things, that Nick had come to their rescue once more, Isabel knew she had to keep Boyd's full attention on her.

"I can understand why you might hate Father," Isabel said as she saw him creeping into position behind Boyd. "But why us? We're all victims of his ambition, Boyd. All three of us."

"Don't compare your lives to mine. Don't you dare!"

Aware that Louise stiffened, Isabel knew she, too, had spotted Nick. She reached back surreptitiously and found her sister's hand. Louise squeezed back in acknowledgment.

"Did you want for anything, Boyd?" Isabel mentally counted the yards between him and Nick. "Food, clothing, a roof over your head?"

"No, what does that prove?"

"That Father thought as much of you as he did of us. And by the way, why Cummings? Why aren't you using your mother's name, Bower?" she asked as those yards of separation dwindled and Nick signaled her to be ready.

"Mama had a short-lived marriage. The man's name ended up on the birth certifi—"

Before he could complete the word, Nick was on him, knocking his hand upward as the gun went off. The men danced under the metal structure until Nick got a grip on Boyd's hand and banged it against a support. The gun dropped to the ground. And when they turned away again, trading ineffectual punches at the close distance, Louise shot forward and grabbed it.

"Louise, no!" Isabel cried as her sister put the weapon in both hands and held it out toward the dueling duo. "Put down the gun!"

Louise's hands were shaking and Isabel was terrified the gun would go off and the bullet would find its way to an unsuspecting Nick. The two men were impossibly close.

"Please, Louise," she begged, "for me. Put the gun down for me."

Then Louise seemed to get hold of herself and lowered the gun. Isabel rushed to her, took the weapon from her hands and wrapped her arms around her sister's shaking shoulders.

"He can't hurt us now," Isabel reassured her.

"What if he hurts Nick?"

"Nick can take care of himself. He learned how a long time ago."

Even so, she watched carefully to be sure, as Nick pushed Boyd away and drew back his arm. He delivered the punch with so much force that Boyd spun and fell forward, trying to grab on to a support and missing.

Even as Boyd's forehead glanced off the edge and he slumped to the ground, Isabel heard the commotion out front. Undoubtedly someone had heard the gun go off.

Suddenly, two cops burst through the gangway, guns drawn.

"Nobody move!" one yelled.

15

―――――

"INCREDIBLE, ISN'T IT?" Nick muttered, taking another slug of coffee at the early-morning ritual meeting with Annie and Helen at the cybercafé. "I lose the love of my life twice, both times to the same man—her father."

The irony being that she wasn't even related to the man, not that he wanted to go into that.

"If you truly love Isabel, you have to fight for her," Annie told him.

"I would, if only I could be sure she was free of the senator for good."

He feared that once Isabel confronted him with his duplicity, the senator would use her feelings against her, find a way to trick her into staying loyal to him.

"It doesn't matter," he muttered, downing the rest of his coffee. "I can live without her."

"You big jerk!" Helen gave him a furious scowl. "Now is not the time to let something slide off your back. At least not Isabel Grayson. She isn't just some woman. She's the woman for *you*. Now, get off your butt and do something to get her into your life permanently."

"Who died and made you boss?"

''No, not this time,'' Helen said. ''You're not sucking me into some verbal battle to distract me. I'm serious. You ought to be glad you have something personal to fight for instead of just professional woes.''

''Where is this coming from?'' Nick asked. ''Part of the idea of running our own businesses was to get away from ulcer-producing jobs.''

''Right. But that was before the Hot Zone.''

''The Hot Zone?'' Nick echoed.

''The Hot Zone,'' Annie clarified, ''is a national chain of coffee houses.''

Helen explained, ''They're planning on opening several in Chicago, starting with this neighborhood. If I don't do something to stop it from happening, I'm ruined.''

''So you're planning on what?''

''I would have a face-to-face with the owner himself if I thought it would do any good. But I've heard about this Luke DeVries, how he smiles and nods, makes you think he's with you...and then just goes ahead and does what he wants, anyway. Maybe I can get local businesspeople to picket the area and then the politicians—''

''Uh-huh,'' Annie interrupted.

Silence. Annie's Attic had been picketed several times when it first opened due to its erotic products, and she was obviously still sensitive about the issue.

''Sorry,'' Helen muttered. ''We were talking about Nick.''

Annie nodded and turned back to him. ''Helen and

Nate and I all want you to be happy.'' A grin spread from ear to ear, undoubtedly because *she* was happy. Suddenly she shot a hand adorned with a sizable diamond in front of his face. ''Nate's going to make an honest woman of me.''

''You and Nate are getting married?'' Nick got up, rounded the table and pulled Annie to her feet for a hug. ''I hope you realize you have me to thank.''

''Next thing you know,'' Helen said, ''he'll be taking credit for Christmas, too.''

Kissing Annie on both cheeks, Nate ignored Helen. ''Don't let Isabel get away,'' she said softly.

''I'll sleep on it,'' he promised. ''If I can sleep after that jolt of caffeine.''

Helen groaned and rolled her eyes. ''Don't blow it, Novak, or I'll…well, just don't blow it.''

He bent over and kissed Helen on the cheek, as well.

She looked nonplussed, while Annie grinned harder. Nick grinned back and gave her a thumbs-up, but inside he was seething with pain.

Sleep on it, indeed. What was there to sleep on?

The cops had come in gangbusters. Since they hadn't found him home, they'd been about to leave when Boyd's gun had gone off, which then brought them running to the rapid-transit station.

After a cursory questioning, the cops had brought the four of them to the police station to sort it all out. Once there, Isabel had kept some distance between them and focused her attention on her sister. Every so often she'd looked his way, but when he'd caught her staring, she'd directed her gaze past his shoulder. He hadn't been able to tell what the hell she'd been thinking.

Once the police had taken their statements and they were free to go, however, he'd asked her. A veil had descended over her lovely face and Isabel had simply replied, "I need to see my father before this all explodes in his face."

Big surprise!

As he climbed up to his studio, Nick wondered how much longer Isabel would have to sell herself before the senator gave her what she so obviously needed from him.

"WHAT IS IT? GOOD NEWS at last, I hope?" Senator William Grayson demanded as he entered the town house study early Sunday morning. "Is the problem contained?"

Louise…a problem to be contained…

Turning from the window of the place that had been her only home for twenty-eight years, Isabel faced the man she'd called Father all her life and wondered if he felt anything for anyone. She supposed he had feelings for Amber Bower, although he'd betrayed her, as well.

He'd sold himself for his political ambition. Her mother had sold herself to get a father for her child. And the Bower woman had sold herself to stay with the man she loved, Isabel supposed. Or perhaps she had simply wanted to be kept in comfortable circumstances.

Despite what she knew now, Isabel still didn't understand. How could this man have lived a lie for so many years without falling into it? She'd been a vulnerable child and then a vulnerable young woman who'd been tangled in his lies. What had run through his head every time she'd called him Father?

"Do you feel nothing for me?" she asked.

He tightened the belt around his robe and scowled at her. "Is that why you got me out of bed so early on a Saturday morning? To quiz me?"

A question with a question. Something she'd been guilty of more times than she cared to remember when she hadn't wanted to answer a query.

"Actually, I'm here to warn you. But, first, know that Louise is safe and with Mother at a hotel…that is if you care anything for her."

"Of course I care. She's my daughter."

Isabel swallowed hard. "And Boyd is under arrest."

Not even skipping a beat, he asked, "For what?"

"Attempted murder. Louise and I stood between you and him and he couldn't take that anymore."

Despite the reasons Boyd had spouted about rising in the Democratic party, Isabel knew they were only a symptom of the real disease—Senator William Grayson. Boyd had been driven to prove his worth to his father. Unfortunately, he'd used drugs to bolster his ego, or his bravery. She thought perhaps his being under the influence had allowed him to commit what otherwise would have been insane acts.

"What do you know?" he growled.

"Everything," Isabel said. "Well, as much as Boyd knew. How could you raise a child as your own, Senator, without ever really being her father?"

"Senator?"

"Let's be honest."

A heartbeat passed. "But people don't know that I'm not your real father," he said, confirming it. "If we put our heads together, we can spin this, Isabel—"

"Damn everyone else!" And damn him, though she didn't say it. "People *will* know everything once the media gets hold of this story. I'm not going to do a thing to stop it because I'm no longer working for you."

Even so, if he showed her just one sign of affection or regret, she might weaken and do what she could before she left this place for good. She watched as his expression turned stormy. Of course, he never failed in one way—never failed to disappoint her.

His face had grown red and his eyes bulged. "You can't do this to me!"

"I didn't, Senator," she said, knowing it to be true. "I'm afraid you did this to yourself."

With that, she headed for the study door, intending to walk out of his political career—and his life—forever. Her hand was on the doorknob when he called after her.

"Proud of yourself, are you?"

Isabel turned for one last look at the father she'd never had. "Yes. Finally, I am."

BAM-BAM-BAM...

Nick dragged himself up out of the depths of sleep and eyed his clock. It was 6:00 a.m. Who the hell was banging at his door at this early hour?

Bam-bam-bam...

"Yeah, put a lid on it!" he shouted as he rolled out of bed. "I'm coming."

Realizing he was nude, Nick swept up his jeans from the floor and stepped into the legs as he walked. He couldn't bear the damn banging. His head already felt big enough, thanks to the half bottle of vodka he'd downed so he could sleep. He fumbled with the zipper as he unlocked the door and swung it open.

And damn if Isabel Grayson's gaze didn't zero in on that very spot.

"Nick, don't dress up for me." She raised one perfectly arched eyebrow at him.

She was dressed, coiffed and made-up as if she were ready to go before the cameras.

"What can I do for you this time, Isabel?" he growled, defiantly leaving the zipper partially undone.

"You can invite me in."

She looked as cool and pulled together and sleekly beautiful as she had the day she'd sought him out. Her suit today was a soft blue the same shade as her eyes, and the skirt was short enough to make his imagination soar right under it.

Nick took a step back and she swept by him with excruciating slowness, as if she wanted to make certain he would catch her scent. Her usual musk was heightened with spice. Ginger, he thought, looking down into cleavage that made his mouth go dry.

"So, what is it, Isabel?" he asked, his grip on the doorknob strong enough to tear it off.

She turned and tilted her head so that a stray strand of hair swept her cheek. "I wanted to thank you, Nick," she said sweetly.

Yesterday she'd left him high and dry and today she was acting all coy.

"Louise is all right, then?"

"She will be. We've checked into a hotel. Mother is there now, just temporarily," Isabel added. "She has her own life to worry about."

As if that could be more important than her daughters. But nothing could surprise him now.

And why was he feeling sorry for Isabel? She'd made all her own choices, including the one that left him behind when she decided she needed to talk to the old man.

"I intend to make a life for Louise and me," she continued. "Our own apartment will be a start. Then she'll go away to college in the fall."

"What about you, Isabel?"

"I called it quits with the senator before coming here. And last night, when I couldn't sleep, I spent several hours organizing my thoughts about the story I want to tell. After I write it and, I hope, sell it, I'm not sure which direction to take. Money's not an issue at the moment, so I thought I would volunteer at Haven and see where the need is greatest."

She wanted to work at the drop-in center? For free? "You're serious?"

"As a heart attack," she agreed lightly.

Realizing Isabel hadn't said anything about her personal feelings concerning the man she'd been led to believe was her father, Nick thought she must be suffering under a brave front. One he didn't want to wreck for her. When she was ready, she would tell him.

"So what do you want with me, Isabel?" he asked softly. "If you had simply wanted to thank me, you could have called."

"Yes, well…there *is* a little matter of a revealing videotape…."

"Ah, the videotape." He should have known. He would have erased it if she'd asked, but no doubt she wouldn't trust him to do so. "I'll get it." He turned away, muttering, "I knew there had to be some self-motivated reason for your coming here."

Following, she said, "I'm only human."

As was he. His gut tightened as he went to the camcorder to get her the damn videotape, wondering if this was the last time he would see her alone.

"Wait!" she said as he was about to press Eject. "Start recording, would you? I want to add something to that tape."

Nick whipped around to find her perched on the hot seat, one leg crossed over the other, revealing a flesh-colored lace garter belt that she might have bought from Annie. She was wearing thigh-high stockings rather than panty hose.

Ignoring his instant hard-on, Nick turned back to

the equipment and did as she requested. "So, Isabel, what is it you have to say?"

"Not a lot, but it's important."

On the monitor, he saw her undo the top button of her blouse.

"I don't know if I'm so guilty for what I did... dumping you, I mean...but I admit that I was a fool when it came to trying to please my so-called father," she said, unbuttoning the next two. "I wasted so much time when I have so much I want to give." She freed the tails of her blouse from the skirt and let it hang in open invitation. "And I want to give it all to you, Nick Novak, because I love you with all my heart."

That's all Nick needed to hear to propel him toward her. Damn! That bra looked amazingly see-through. Or was there a bra? Smiling, she uncrossed her legs and he could see that she wasn't wearing any panties.

She wasn't wearing any underwear at all!

Nick grinned and unzipped his jeans as he focused on her face. On her lips.

"That apartment you're going to get...um, when Louise leaves for school, won't you feel a little lost wandering through all those rooms alone?"

She licked her lips. "Not if I have *you* to keep me company."

"You want to live together?"

"I thought you would never ask."

Nick could tell she was keeping her tone light, her words double-edged, just in case. "I love you, too, Isabel Grayson. I always have and I always will. And nothing would make me happier than to start a life with you.''

He kissed her to seal the deal, and she wrapped her long, lovely legs around his back. As he levered her in the hot seat so he could better get to her, the red eye on the camera seemed to wink at him.

The tape was still rolling....

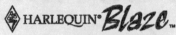

More fabulous reading from
the Queen of Sizzle!

LORI FOSTER

with

Forever and Always

Back by popular demand are the scintillating stories of
Gabe and Jordan Buckhorn. They're gorgeous, sexy
and single...at least for now!

Available wherever books are sold—September 2002.

And look for Lori's **brand-new** single title,
CASEY in early 2003

HARLEQUIN®
Makes any time special ®

Visit us at www.eHarlequin.com

PHLF-2

This is the family reunion you've been waiting for!

TRUEBLOOD
Christmas

JASMINE CRESSWELL
TARA TAYLOR QUINN
& KATE HOFFMANN

deliver three brand new Trueblood, Texas stories.

After many years, Major Brad Henderson is released from prison, exonerated after almost thirty years for a crime he didn't commit. His mission: to be reunited with his three daughters. How to find them? Contact Dylan Garrett of the Finders Keepers Detective Agency!

Look for it in November 2002.

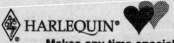

Fall in _Love_
THIS WINTER
WITH
HARLEQUIN BOOKS!

In October 2002 look for these special volumes
led by _USA TODAY_ bestselling authors,
and receive MOULIN ROUGE on video*!

*Retail value of $14.98 U.S. Mail-in offer. Two proofs of purchase required.
Limited time offer. Offer expires 3/31/03.

See inside these books for details.

Own MOULIN ROUGE on video!

_This exciting promotion
is available at your
favorite retail outlet._

Only from
HARLEQUIN®
Makes any time special ®